All I Want for Christmas is a Rogue

REGENCY HEARTS AFLAME: BENEATH THE FALLING SNOW, LOVE BLAZES

AMANDA MARIEL

One

⁂

Nicolas Winters leaned over the billiards table, eyes narrowed, and lined up his cue with practiced precision. With a deft stroke, the red ball rolled smoothly into the corner pocket. A triumphant grin spread across his face as he looked up at his friends.

"Well played, Winters," James Barton, Viscount Blackwood, drawled, taking his cue in hand. "But do not get too cocky. I believe it is my turn now."

As James lined up his shot, Johnathan Hargate, Duke of Hargate, crossed his arms and studied the table. "I must say, Blackwood, your skills have improved considerably since our days at Eton. I recall you being quite terrible at this game."

James chuckled, taking his shot and sinking the ball in quick succession. "We all start somewhere,

Hargate, though I seem to remember you spent more time buried in books than with a cue in hand."

"Sharpening the mind is hardly a waste of time," Johnathan said good-naturedly, "unlike wasting away in idle pursuits."

Nicolas smirked. "Come now, what's life without a little idle pursuit now and then? All work and no play, as they say."

The clack of billiard balls punctuated their banter as James took another shot. He straightened with a self-satisfied grin. "Idle pursuits, my friends, have their merits."

Nicolas laughed and shook his head. These private moments with his friends were rare and cherished, a respite from the expectations and pretenses of London society. Here, in the relative privacy of Blackwood's country estate, they could let their guards down and simply enjoy each other's company.

As he reached for his glass of brandy, a sound outside caught his attention—the unmistakable rhythm of hoofbeats growing louder. Frowning, he glanced toward the window, noting the ominous clouds gathering in the grey sky.

Johnathan set down his glass, his gaze following Nicolas's. "It would appear a storm is coming. The sky looks rather ominous."

"It is likely just a messenger," James remarked, though a flicker of unease crossed his face. "Could be news from London."

Nicolas felt the weight of dread settle in his gut. News from London was rarely good, but what else could it be? They were not expecting anyone and given the time of year and weather, it was not likely to be one of their peers. He watched as the new arrival disappeared into the house, then rode back down the drive a few minutes later. Whatever it was about, they would know soon enough.

"It is your turn, Winters," Hargate said.

Nicolas moved back to the billiards table, cue in hand. As he leaned over to line up his shot, a sudden burst of footsteps echoed from the corridor, and all three men turned toward the door.

The heavy oak door swung open. Selina, Viscountess Blackwood, stepped into the room, her face flushed from her brisk walk through the manor. In her hand, she held a folded letter, concern filling her gaze.

"Nicolas," she said, her voice steady but urgent, "I was in the entry hall when this letter arrived. The messenger said it was of the utmost importance, so I brought it myself."

His stomach clenched. He strode forward and took the letter.

The room grew still as he broke the wax seal, then unfolded the paper. His friends watched him, the air thick with tension. Nicolas's eyes scanned the words, his heart sinking with each line. He lowered the letter, his face set in grim determination.

"What is it?" James asked, breaking the silence.

Nicolas's jaw tightened. "It is Joslyn. Lord Forge has compromised her in public. She's being pressured into marrying him—she will be ruined if she refuses."

Selina gasped, her hand flying to her mouth. "Your sister? Oh, Nicolas, I am so sorry."

Nicolas crushed the letter in his fist, his mind racing. "I must leave for London immediately. I will not let that bastard ruin her life."

Johnathan stepped forward, his expression dark with concern. "You can not ride out in this weather. The storm is nearly upon us, and the roads will be dangerous."

"I do not have a choice," Nicolas said, urgency clawing at him. "Joslyn's future is at stake. I can hardly sit here and do nothing while that libertine forces her into marriage." He dropped his cue stick on the billiards table, a resounding thwack resonating through the room. "He cares nothing for her."

Selina stepped closer, her brow furrowed with

worry. "The storm will be treacherous. You could get injured, or worse. Please, at least wait until the weather clears."

"There is no time." His voice softened as he glanced at her, seeing the genuine concern etched across her face. "Every moment I wait, is another moment Forge has to manipulate her. Marriage to that scoundrel would be far worse than social ruin. I cannot delay."

Johnathan frowned, clearly unconvinced. "You are a skilled rider, but no man can outrun a storm. At least take precautions. Do not be reckless."

Selina nodded. "Your sister needs you alive and well."

Though their concern warmed his heart, it was not enough to change his course. "I will be careful, but I must go. I can not let Forge ruin Joslyn's life."

Selina's gaze lingered on him, her voice full of worry. "Promise me you will send word when you arrive safely."

"I will," Nicolas said, offering her a small smile. "Thank you."

With a nod to his friends, Nicolas turned and left the room, the weight of responsibility pressing heavily on his shoulders. He knew the journey ahead would be fraught with danger, but there was no alternative. Joslyn needed him.

As he reached the stables, James caught up to him, his eyes filled with determination. "Nicolas, let me come with you. I will have my coach readied at once."

Nicolas paused, tempted by the offer. He pulled his greatcoat closer to block the wind. Traveling with a friend in a well-equipped coach would be safer. "I appreciate it, James, but this is my burden. I will not drag you into it. Besides, a horse would be both faster and better able to navigate the mounting drifts."

James's frown deepened. "You would be better protected from the storm in a coach."

Nicolas clapped a hand on his friend's shoulder. "It is merely a winter squall. I have survived worse, James. I will be fine."

After a long, assessing look, James sighed. "Very well. But remember that no man is invincible, and act accordingly."

"You have my word," Nicolas assured him, reaching for his reins.

James nodded, stepping back as Nicolas mounted his horse. "We will be waiting for word."

With one last glance at his friends, Nicolas spurred his horse into the approaching storm. Soon snow swirled around him, the wind howling as he rode through the icy landscape. The cold bit at his skin, but he hardly felt it—his mind consumed with thoughts of Joslyn.

Forge's actions were unforgivable. Though aware of the man's reputation, Nicolas never imagined he would stoop so low. The no good scoundrel had manipulated the situation to force a marriage, knowing full well what the consequences would be for Joslyn.

Nicolas's blood boiled at the thought. He would stop Forge, whatever it took. He urged his horse faster, the wind whipping at his coat, but the storm was closing in. Snow fell thickly, obscuring the path ahead, and the road grew slick with ice.

Still, Nicolas pressed on, pushing his horse through the deepening snowdrifts. Joslyn's happiness depended on him reaching London in time to save her. He could not afford to fail.

Suddenly, a deafening crack of thunder split the air, the ground shaking beneath him. His horse reared in fright, nearly throwing him from the saddle. Nicolas fought to regain control, his heart pounding in his chest. "Easy, boy," he said, trying to calm the panicked animal.

With a wild snort, it bolted toward the trees, its hooves slipping on the icy ground. Nicolas leaned forward on his horse, his hands gripping the reins as the animal plunged ahead, blind with fear.

"Damn it," Nicolas cursed under his breath as he struggled to steer the horse back onto the road. They were veering dangerously close to the dense tree line.

The wind howled around them, the plump snowflakes creating a thick, blinding sheet. His pulse raced as he fought to regain control, pulling hard on the reins to slow his horse. But just as the animal responded, another crack of thunder split the sky.

The beast reared again, and this time, Nicolas lost his grip. His body lurched forward, and before he could react, his forehead collided with a low-hanging branch. Pain exploded in his skull.

He hit the ground with a heavy thud, knocking the breath out of him. His head spun violently, the world around him a blur of white and grey.

A fleeting image of Joslyn, pale with fear, her future in limbo, flashed in his mind—a reminder of what was at stake.

Then darkness claimed him.

Two

L ady Emily Fairchild set down her teacup, the soft clink of china barely audible over the mounting howl of the wind outside. The frost-laced windows of Greystone Manor framed a bleak view. The snow, which had drifted lazily this morning, now gathered strength as the storm closed in. A chill slipped through the cracks of the old house, making the candle flames flicker.

"The storm shows no sign of letting up, my lady," Brinks, her butler, said as he entered the room. His silver hair gleamed in the dim light, and his posture was, as always, impeccable. "The sky is quite foreboding."

Emily glanced at him, a polite smile curving her lips. "Yes, Brinks, I have noticed. Let us hope it does not prove too severe."

Yet, despite her composed words, a nervous flutter tightened her chest. A storm in the countryside could mean days of isolation, and with the winter winds gaining force, even Greystone's sturdy walls felt fragile against nature's wrath.

"Shall I have the staff bring in more wood for the fires, my lady?" Brinks inquired.

"Yes, see to it." She rose from her seat. "Ensure the stables are in order as well. We must prepare for the weather to worsen."

"Indeed, my lady." Brinks offered a respectful nod.

Emily moved toward the window, her pink gown whispering softly across the polished floor. The wind had picked up, its low moan building into a relentless howl that rattled the panes. She pressed her fingers to the cold glass, watching the snowflakes multiply until the world outside became a white, swirling void.

It had been three years since Thomas's passing, and yet the weight of responsibility still rested heavily on her. She had a duty to preserve the estate until her son came of an age to take over. Each decision, no matter how small, felt like a test she had not fully prepared for. Today, the air in the house felt charged, not just with the storm, but with something else. Something she could not quite name.

"My lady?" Brinks's voice pulled her from her thoughts.

She turned, her expression composed once more. "I am quite well, Brinks. I will see to the kitchen. Please ensure the rest of the preparations are in place."

Brinks bowed and left the room, his footsteps echoing down the hall. As Emily made her way through the manor, the eerie sound of the wind seemed to follow her, winding through the corridors like a living thing. The walls, usually so familiar, felt oppressively large and empty today, and a creeping sense of unease settled deeper into her bones.

"It is only a storm," she whispered, clutching the folds of her skirt, her fingers cool against the silk. "Nothing more."

As she approached the kitchen, a burst of commotion erupted from the direction of the servants' entrance. Raised voices, hurried and urgent, cut through the air, muffled only slightly by the thick walls of the manor.

Her pulse quickened as she hurried toward the source of the noise, gathering her skirts as she rounded the corner. There, in the back corridor, she found Mrs. Thatcher, her usually composed house-keeper, waving her hands as she directed the foot-men, Marks and Willy. Both men stood dripping wet, snow clinging to their boots, their faces flushed from the cold.

"What is going on?" Emily asked, her voice sharp and authoritative.

Marks stepped forward, his head bowed. "My lady, we found a man collapsed in the snow. Couldn't leave him out there."

"A man? In this storm?" Emily's pulse quickened. "Where is he now?" she asked, her voice rising with urgency.

"In the wagon, my lady," Willy said, his breath still coming in heavy puffs. "There was a riderless horse standing nearby. We calmed the horse and lead it to the stables. Would have taken the man to the stables, too, but he looks to be a gentleman. He's in a bad way, my lady. We feared he was dead."

"Bring him inside at once. Take him to the blue guest room. Mrs. Thatcher, have blankets, hot water, and broth prepared immediately." Her tone left no room for hesitation.

The servants sprang into action, but as Emily watched them carry out her orders, her thoughts raced. Who was this stranger? What had brought him to collapse on her property in the middle of a snowstorm?

She followed Marks and Willy up the grand staircase as they carried the man between them. When

Marks and Willy laid him on the bed, Emily stepped closer, studying him—tall, broad-shouldered, his fine clothing sodden and disheveled. His face, though pallid from the cold, bore the unmistakable features of nobility, yet there was something rugged about him. Something untamed.

Her gaze moved to the angry, swollen bump on his forehead. Her breath caught as she studied the injury, the surrounding skin darkening into a bruise. A thin trail of dried blood had run from the cut near his hairline, stark against his pale complexion.

After a moment's hesitation, she reached out, her fingers hovering just above the wound. It looked as though he had fallen hard, perhaps hit his head on something sharp. His dark hair, damp with melted snow, clung to his forehead, framing his strong, aristocratic features. Her eyes lingered on the sharp planes of his face, trying to pinpoint what it was about him that felt so familiar.

Emily drew in a slow breath, allowing herself to study him further. His nose was straight and finely shaped, his jaw strong with a hint of stubble that lent him a rakish air. His lips, though pale, were full, and she noticed the shadow of a dimple at one corner, hinting at a smile that might once have been quick to form. There was something disconcerting in the contrast of his current vulnerability and the clear strength of his features.

"Who are you?" she asked. "And what happened to you?"

Mrs. Thatcher bustled into the room with the requested supplies, directing the others as they removed the man's wet coat, boots, and breeches, piled blankets atop him, and placed heated bricks by his feet. A fire roared to life in the hearth, casting a warm glow over the room.

"My lady," Mrs. Thatcher said, "should I send for Dr. Whiteside?"

"The roads are quickly becoming impassable," Marks said.

Emily shook her head. "We will have to manage on our own. I will not put my staff in danger."

Emily watched the unconscious man closely. There was an almost unsettling recognition, though it danced at the edge of her mind. Had they met before? Or was it merely the sharpness of his features that made him recognizable?

She reached out, almost instinctively, to brush a lock of dark hair from his forehead. The moment her fingers touched his skin, a jolt of awareness shot through her, startling her. She withdrew her hand, her pulse quickening.

"He's quite a handsome one, is he not?" Mrs. Thatcher remarked, amusement lacing her tone.

Emily felt warmth creep up her neck. "I had not noticed," she lied, though her racing pulse said otherwise.

Mrs. Thatcher gave a knowing smile. "Begging your pardon, my lady, but do you recognize him? He does look to be a gentleman of some standing."

Emily studied him again, brow furrowed. "There is… something familiar, but I cannot say for certain." Her gaze lingered on the bump at his temple. "We will have to wait until he wakes to learn who he is. For now, let us ensure he is comfortable."

"Perhaps we should send word to Millbrook once the storm passes," Mrs. Thatcher said. "Someone may be searching for him."

"Yes," Emily said, though her thoughts were already elsewhere. "But for now, we must do our best to care for him."

With the fire blazing and the stranger settled, Mrs. Thatcher moved to pull the blankets higher around his shoulders. "Shall we leave him to rest, my lady?"

Emily nodded. "Indeed. Marks, Willy—one of you must remain with him at all times. Should he wake, inform me immediately."

Both footmen bowed, replying in unison, "Yes, my lady."

Hours later, Emily sat before the fire in her bedchamber as the snow outside intensified, rattling the windows with a fury she had not expected. Yet, it was not just the weather that unsettled her.

Who was the man in her guest room? And why did he stir a strange sense of recognition deep within her?

She moved to the window, her breath fogging the glass as she stared into the endless swirl of snow. The world beyond the manor had disappeared, buried beneath the storm's relentless grip. She sighed as she turned from the window.

The storm did not just bring snow to her door—it brought change.

And change, she knew, could bring dangers far greater than any storm.

Three

〜

T he pale winter sun filtered through the drawn curtains, casting a soft glow across the stranger's feverish face. Emily stood at his bedside, brow furrowed with concern. Two days had passed since they found him unconscious in the snow. Though the fever had not worsened, it had yet to break. His features, still sharp and undeniably handsome, were marred by the fever's flush, his dark hair tousled against the pillow from the restless thrashing of the previous night.

Emily had spent countless hours caring for him and urging him to wake as the storm raged outside. This morning Marks informed her the roads were blanketed in knee deep snow. Willy added some drifts were waist high. Though the snow had stopped falling, they were well and truly snowed-in.

"Penny," Emily called softly, turning to her maid. "Fetch fresh linens and cool water. We must continue to do everything in our power to make our patient comfortable."

"Yes, my lady." Penny offered a quick curtsy before leaving the room.

Her gaze returned to the man lying so still, a persistent sense of familiarity tugging at her. She was sure they had crossed paths before, though the details eluded her. There was something about his face—his strong jawline, the dark sweep of hair across his brow—that tugged at her memory. She was almost certain they had met before, though where or when escaped her entirely.

Gently, she reached out and laid her hand upon his forehead. His skin was still burning, though mercifully no hotter than it had been. She allowed herself a small sigh of relief. The fever had held steady, and for now, that was enough. Still, as her hand rested there, she felt an unsettling sensation—a quiet awareness of the softness of his skin, the steady pulse beneath, and the faint scent of bay rum that clung to him despite his condition.

Her breath caught, and she quickly withdrew her hand, disconcerted by the flutter of emotion that stirred within her.

"You must wake soon, sir," she said. "There are many questions I should like to ask."

For a fleeting moment, his eyelids fluttered at the sound of her voice, though they did not open. His body remained as still as before, his chest rising and falling with each laboured breath. Emily settled into the chair beside the bed, her gaze never leaving his face.

It was improper, of course, to sit here alone with a man, a stranger no less, but propriety had always been a distant second to compassion in her mind.

She wondered what kind of man he was. His fine clothing suggested he was a gentleman, though there was something about him—something decidedly unrefined—that did not sit neatly with the image of a polished aristocrat. And then there was the matter of his being found in a snowstorm, alone, near her estate. It made no sense. If he were from the local gentry, she would have known him. But she did not.

Or did she?

A faint knock on the door interrupted her thoughts, and Penny returned, her arms laden with fresh linens. Behind her, Marks followed with a basin of cool water.

"Thank you, Penny," Emily said, rising from her seat. "I will check his wound after you have finished. I have faith that, with care, he will recover."

Penny curtsied again, her face tight with concentration as she set about changing the linens. Marks worked silently beside her. The room filled with the soft rustling of fabric and the occasional crackle from the fire.

As they worked, Emily's thoughts drifted back to the previous days. The storm had been fierce, relentless, and when the footmen had brought this man into her home, she had not hesitated. It was her duty, her instinct, to care for those in need. But now, after two days of waiting, the uncertainty of his identity gnawed at her.

"Marks," she said as the footman finished his task. "That will do for now. Thank you."

Marks bowed slightly before backing from the room, his heavy footsteps fading down the corridor. Emily turned to Penny, her gaze thoughtful.

"Penny, I had hoped we might not need to resort to such measures, but I believe the time has come." Her voice was steady but laced with concern. "Please search his coat pockets. He has been unconscious for too long, and we must know who he is. If there is anything to identify him, we must find it."

Penny hesitated for a moment, her brow furrowing, but then she hastened to the chair where the stranger's belongings were laid. She rifled through the pockets of his coat, her fingers deft but respectful. A moment later, she produced a small collection of items: a silver pocket watch, a few coins, and a folded letter.

Emily's breath caught in her throat as she took the letter from Penny's outstretched hand. The parchment appeared worn and creased, as though someone had folded and refolded it many times. Her fingers trembled slightly as she unfolded it, her curiosity mingling with shame, for she knew it was wrong to invade his privacy. Despite the pang of guilt, she proceeded.

"My dear Nicolas," she read softly, her voice barely above a whisper. "I implore you to make haste to London. The matter is of utmost urgency, and your presence is required to—" She stopped, her breath catching. A dark stain obscured the rest of the letter, likely from the snow that had soaked through his clothing.

Emily's heart lurched as recognition sank in. This was *that* Nicolas Winters, the rake whose name had graced more than a few scandal sheets. And now, he lay unconscious in her home, vulnerable and at her mercy.

"Penny," Emily said, her voice tight with recognition. "I believe we are hosting none other than Mr.

Nicolas Winters. Scandalous son of the Earl of Quinton."

The maid's eyes widened in shock. "The second son of the Earl?" she gasped. "Mr. Winters, the notorious rake that even servants whisper about?"

"Indeed," Emily said, her gaze fixed on his face. The man before her bore a striking resemblance to the Earl of Quinton, but she had never imagined this to be that Nicolas Winters, the charming rogue whose escapades had fuelled many a scandal in London. The man in her guest room seemed so far removed from the lively figure described in society's gossip—so vulnerable, so far from the carefree libertine she had heard about.

Penny looked at her, wide-eyed. "What shall we do, my lady?"

Emily straightened, her resolve hardening. "We shall continue to care for him, as we have been. Mr. Winters is in need of our help, and we shall provide it, regardless of his reputation. Besides, his father is an acquaintance of my late husband. It is our duty."

Penny nodded, her face pale but composed. "Yes, my lady."

As Penny quietly left the room, Emily returned to her seat by the bed. Her gaze lingered on Nicolas's face, her thoughts spinning. She had never met him before—at least, not formally—but his reputation had preceded him. She had heard the whispers, the stories of his exploits in London, the tales of his charm and mischief. But now, as she looked at him, none of that seemed to matter. He was a man in need, nothing more.

And yet, there was something unsettling about the situation, something that made her heart race whenever she thought of the name Nicolas Winters. She had always prided herself on seeing the best in people, on offering kindness where others might judge. But this... this was different. She could not ignore the feeling that she was treading on dangerous ground.

"Oh, Mr. Winters," she said as she pressed a cool cloth to his brow. "What trouble have you found yourself in this time?"

As if in response to her voice, his eyelids fluttered again. Emily held her breath, watching as his eyes slowly opened, unfocused and glazed with fever. He blinked several times, his brow furrowing as he tried to make sense of his surroundings.

"Where..." His voice was hoarse, barely above a whisper. His gaze moved sluggishly from the fire to the tapestries on the walls before finally settling on her.

Emily's heart quickened. She reached for the glass of water on the nightstand and leaned forward, her voice soft but steady. "You are in Gilford Manor, Mr. Winters. Here, sip some water. It will help."

With care, she lifted his head and held the glass to his lips. He sipped, his gaze never leaving hers. When he had taken enough, she set the glass aside and gently lowered him back onto the pillows.

"Lady... Gilford?" he rasped, his voice stronger now, though still rough from disuse.

Emily offered him a small smile. "Indeed. It seems fate has brought you to my doorstep this December."

He tried to push himself up, but Emily laid a hand on his shoulder, gently pressing him back. "No, you must rest. You have been through quite an ordeal, and your body needs time to recover."

He frowned, confusion flickering in his eyes. "How... how did I come to be here?"

"Two of my footmen found you near the road," Emily explained, settling back in her chair. "You were unconscious in a snowbank with a rather nasty bump on your head. A horse was nearby."

Nicolas winced, raising a hand to his temple. His fingers brushed against the cool cloth, and he let out a soft groan of pain.

"Easy now," Emily said, leaning forward once

more. "You have had a terrible fall, but you are safe now. Your horse is in my stable and well cared for. You need only to rest."

He nodded weakly, though a flicker of stubbornness remained in his captivating green eyes. "Thank you, Lady Gilford," he said, his voice laced with the remnants of his charm as exhaustion took over. "It seems… I am… in your debt."

Emily busied herself adjusting the blankets, her fingers working with practiced ease while her heart betrayed her with a traitorous flutter. She had heard many things about Nicolas Winters, most of them scandalous, but nothing had prepared her for the man himself.

"It was nothing," she replied, her tone even. "I could not leave you at the mercy of the storm. You are fortunate my footmen found you when they did."

He chuckled, though the sound was strained. "Fortunate indeed." His eyes closed for a heartbeat before he added, "Though I confess… I remember very little." He drew in a ragged breath. "I suppose I have you to thank for my care?"

Emily glanced at him, her expression softening. "You have my household to thank. Now you must rest until you have fully recovered."

He sighed, the effort of conversation clearly

draining him, though the man seemed too stubborn to care.

"I imagine you are quite curious as to how I came to be in such a state," he said, his voice strained.

"I am," Emily admitted, her tone measured. "But that is a tale for another time. You must regain your strength first."

His gaze lingered on her face, a hint of amusement playing at the corners of his lips. "And here I thought Lady Gilford would be more demanding."

Emily could not suppress a smile. His reputation for charm was well-earned, it seemed. "I have plenty of questions, Mr. Winters, but they can wait. For now, you must rest."

His eyelids fluttered again, the weight of exhaustion pulling him back toward sleep. "As you wish," he said, his voice fading as he drifted into slumber.

Emily remained at his bedside long after he had fallen asleep, her mind filled with thoughts of the scandalous rake now lying in her guest room. He had a reputation, certainly, but beneath the gossip and the scandal, she sensed there was more to him than met the eye.

Eventually, she rose from the chair, her movements quiet as she left the room, closing the door softly behind her.

As she walked down the hall, the familiar weight

of duty settled over her, but this time, a whisper of something new accompanied it. Something unsettling. Her life had been orderly, predictable—but now, with Nicolas Winters under her roof, she could not shake the feeling that it was about to change irrevocably.

Four

〜

The following day, Emily sat at her mahogany writing desk, the soft scratch of quill on parchment filling the air as she reviewed the menus for her son's upcoming school break. The afternoon sunlight streamed through the leaded-glass windows, illuminating the gentle curves of her face.

Cook's roast pheasant with chestnut stuffing, she thought, a soft smile playing on her lips. Mathew always adored that dish. Her heart fluttered with anticipation as she imagined her son's delight upon returning home to his favorite meals.

As Emily continued to pen her notes, her thoughts drifted to Mr. Winters. She wondered about his culinary preferences, her quill hovering above the parchment as she contemplated.

Perhaps he favors hearty stews, she mused, then shook her head with a soft laugh. Oh, Emily, you must not pry into the affairs of your guests.

Yet, as she returned her attention to the menus, she could not quite shake the image of Mr. Winters' teasing eyes and the way they seemed to dance with amusement whenever they conversed. A faint blush rose to her cheeks as she recalled their last encounter. His humor persisted, even as he struggled through his fever.

It would be remiss of her not to ensure his comfort, Emily reasoned, attempting to justify her curiosity. After all, a proper hostess should attend to her guests' needs.

She tapped her quill against her chin, lost in thought. But would it be too forward to inquire directly? Did it matter, given his reputation?

A gentle knock at the door interrupted Emily's internal debate. "My lady," came the voice of her housekeeper. "I have brought you some tea."

"Thank you," Emily replied, grateful for the distraction. As the older woman entered with a silver tray, Emily's gaze fell upon the steaming pot of tea and delicate china cups. An idea struck her.

"Mrs. Thatcher," she began, her tone carefully measured, "I was wondering if you might have noticed any particular preferences Mr. Winters has shown regarding his meals?"

The housekeeper's eyebrows raised slightly, but she answered without hesitation. "Why yes, my lady. The gentleman seems quite partial to Cook's beef Wellington and has praised her apple tarts most enthusiastically."

Emily smiled at this newfound information. "How fortuitous. Thank you, Mrs. Thatcher. You have been most helpful."

As the housekeeper curtsied and left the room, Emily turned back to her planning with renewed vigor. Her quill flew across the parchment, adding Mr. Winters' favorites alongside Mathew's preferred dishes.

"There," she said, satisfaction evident in her voice. "A menu to please both my dear son and our unexpected guest." That is, if Mr. Winters remained for Christmas.

Emily's cheeks warmed at the thought, and she chided herself for such improper musings. Yet, as she glanced out the window at the snow-covered grounds, she could not help but feel a ripple of anticipation for the days to come.

She rose from her desk, her fingers grazing the spine of a leather-bound volume of Shakespearean sonnets. With a decisive nod, she plucked the book from its resting place and cradled it against her chest before grabbing another. The weight of the books steadied her resolve as she made her way toward Mr. Winters' chamber.

As she traversed the corridor, her mind whirred with conflicting thoughts. What if he had remembered why he was traveling? Her pace slowed as she mulled it over. Or worse, what if he had not? How long could she justify withholding the letter? Would he make a hasty departure once he remembered? The carpet muffled her footsteps, but her heartbeat seemed to echo in the quiet hallway.

She paused before his door, drawing a deep breath. "Come now, Emily," she chided herself softly. She was simply checking on an ill guest. Nothing more. Yet, as she raised her hand to knock, she could not ignore the flutter in her stomach.

Her knuckles barely grazed the wood when a muffled voice called out, "Enter, if you must," came the reply, full of mock suffering. "Though I fear I am a lost cause today."

Her lips curved into an involuntary smile at his playful tone. She pushed the door open, stepping into the warm, fire-lit room. "I do hope I am not disturbing your theatrical musings, Mr. Winters." Her gaze moved to his form, propped up against a mound of pillows.

"Lady Gilford," His eyes twinkling with mischief despite his pallor. "you could never be a disturbance. Though I must say, your timing is impeccable. I was just about to pen a sonnet about the abject misery of convalescence."

Emily chuckled, settling into the chair beside his bed. "Well, we cannot have that. I have brought something that might lift your spirits and save us all from your poetic lamentations."

As she held up the book of sonnets, Emily studied his face, searching for any sign of recollection or distress. But his expression remained open and amused, betraying nothing of his mysterious arrival on her property. She bit her lower lip, wondering once more if she should give him the letter.

"Ah, the Bard himself," he said, eyeing the book. "Come to rescue me from my own inferior verses. How kind of you, my lady."

Emily's fingers tightened on the book, her internal debate raging. Should she mention the letter? He was regaining strength, but the roads remained treacherous and he was far from recovered. The moment stretched taut with unspoken words.

Her hesitation was cut short as she noticed a sheen of sweat glistening on his forehead. Concern overtook her conflicted thoughts, and she set the book aside.

"Mr. Winters, you are burning up," she said, her voice laced with worry. She reached for the basin of cool water on the nightstand, wringing out a fresh cloth.

"Am I?" he asked, his eyelids drooping. "And here I thought your radiant presence simply overwhelmed me."

She shook her head, a mix of exasperation and amusement coloring her features. Even in his weakened state, the man's charm seemed irrepressible. She leaned forward, pressing the cool cloth to his forehead.

"I daresay your fever has addled your wits, sir," she said, her tone softening as she tended to him, "but I see your humor is as intact as ever."

His eyes fluttered open at her touch, and a playful smile tugged at the corners of his lips. "On the contrary, my lady," he said, his voice a near whisper. "I find my spirits quite buoyed by your attentions."

Emily felt a warmth creep into her cheeks that had nothing to do with the fire crackling in the hearth. She fussed over the cloth, hoping it would calm both his fever and her own racing heart.

She chided herself for allowing her thoughts to wander. A respectable widow had no business entertaining such notions—yet here she was, her heart betraying her reason with every glance in his direction. It would not do to encourage such flirtations, no matter how charming the man might be.

"You flatter me, Mr. Winters," she said, her voice steady despite her inner turmoil. "But your recovery should be your primary concern."

Emily settled into the chair beside his bed, smoothing her skirts as she sought to regain her composure. She reached for the book she had brought, her fingers tracing the embossed leather cover.

"Perhaps some reading might aid your recovery." She held the books up. "I have brought Wordsworth's 'Lyrical Ballads,' along with Shakespeare's sonnets. I find poetry quite soothing."

Mr. Winters' eyebrows arched playfully. "My dear Lady Gilford, your melodious voice would be far more effective in lulling me to health than mere words on a page."

Emily felt her cheeks warm once more, but she refused to be flustered. "I see your silver tongue remains unaffected by your ailment," she said, a hint of amusement in her voice. "One might think you were trying to charm the entire household."

"Only the parts of it that matter." He winked, then grimaced slightly.

Concern overtook Emily's features. She leaned forward, adjusting the cloth on his forehead. "Come now, Mr. Winters. Let us set aside this banter for the moment. Your health is of paramount importance. You really must be serious."

Determined to regain her composure, she cleared her throat and opened the book.

As she did so, she could not help but wonder how long it would be until he remembered something, or everything, about his mysterious arrival. Surely, if he already had, he would have mentioned it. She pushed the thought aside, focusing instead on the task at hand.

"We shall begin with 'Lines Composed a Few Miles above Tintern Abbey'," she said, her voice taking on a soothing cadence as she read aloud.

Emily's voice filled the room, the soothing words of Wordsworth's poetry flowing from her lips like honey. As she read, her gaze flicked occasionally from the page to Mr. Winters' face, noting the rapt attention with which he listened. His gaze, more often than not dancing with mischief, was now fixed upon her with an intensity that sent a nervous thrill down her spine.

"Five years have passed; five summers, with the length
Of five long winters. And again I hear
These waters, rolling from their mountain-springs

With a soft inland murmur..."

He shifted his gaze to Emily's face. "You read beautifully," he said, his voice low and sincere. "I can almost feel the cool mist of the river on my skin."

As his gaze held hers, a sudden tension passed between them, one that went beyond the surface flirtation. Her pulse quickened, and for a moment, she forgot the lines she had intended to read.

A small smile played at the corners of her mouth. "I am glad you are finding it so immersive. Poetry has always been a balm for my soul in times of distress."

She continued reading, her voice painting vivid pictures of the natural world. As she spoke of "steep and lofty cliffs" and "wild secluded scenes," Emily found herself transported as well, memories of peaceful walks through the estate's grounds flooding her mind.

After some time, her voice began to tire. She finished the poem, placing a silk bookmark between the pages before setting the book aside. Her gaze lingered on Mr. Winters, taking in the sheen of perspiration on his brow.

"I believe it is time to refresh your compress." She reached for the cloth. As she gently dabbed his forehead, she could not help but notice the way his gaze followed her every movement. There was something in his expression—something beyond his usual charm and wit—that made her breath catch.

She leaned in closer, her voice low, soothing. "You must rest now in order to regain your strength." Her warm breath ghosted across his cheek, causing a slight shiver to run through him. "I shall return later with your supper."

He offered a roguish grin, despite his fevered state. "Promise me it will not be gruel, my lady. I fear I might expire from boredom if subjected to such bland fare."

A soft chuckle escaped her lips. "I assure you, sir, our cook takes great pride in her invalid dishes. You will find supper both nourishing and palatable."

"Ah, but will the feast be as delightful as your company?" he said, his voice roughened by fatigue but still carrying that teasing lilt.

She felt a blush creep up her neck. "I am certain you will survive the brief interlude without my presence, Mr. Winters," she said, her tone admonishing but tinged with amusement.

As she rose from her chair, Emily's movements were fluid and graceful. She smoothed her skirts, acutely aware of his gaze following her.

"Until later," she said, offering a small curtsy. "Do try to get some rest."

He nodded, his eyes already beginning to droop.

"I shall dream of poetry and kind-hearted widows," he teased, a ghost of a smile flirting at the edge of his lips.

Emily paused at the door, her hand on the latch. She glanced back, taking in the sight of him, his dark hair tousled against the pillow, chest rising and falling in a steady rhythm. A warmth spread through her, tinged with the quiet thrill of having spent time with him again.

With a gentle click, she closed the door behind her, her thoughts swirling with conflicting emotions. It had been far too long since she had kept company with a man. Since a man had made her blush and long for more...

Her footsteps echoed against the carpeted corridor as she made her way back to her sitting room. Her mind wandered to the gentle cadence of his voice, the way he remained lighthearted, even through his illness. She shook her head, trying to dispel the longing that spread through her at the memory.

This is folly, she thought, her fingers absently tracing the pattern on the wallpaper as she walked. He was not for her.

As she rounded the corner, she nearly collided with her housekeeper.

"Oh! My apologies, Mrs. Thatcher." Emily startled from her reverie.

The older woman's gaze twinkled knowingly. "No harm done, my lady. I trust Mr. Winters is resting comfortably?"

Emily nodded, fighting to keep her expression neutral. "Yes, quite. Though I fear his appetite for teasing remains undiminished by his illness."

Mrs. Thatcher chuckled. "Aye, that one's a charmer, no doubt. Reminds me of my late husband, God rest his soul. I do believe Mr. Winters is a refreshing distraction, my lady."

"Mrs. Thatcher," Emily said, "surely you are not suggesting—"

"I'm suggesting nothing, my lady." The housekeeper grinned. "Merely observing that a bit of laughter does wonders for the spirit, especially during trying times."

Emily sighed, her resolve wavering. "Perhaps, but a respectable widow such as myself—"

"—deserves happiness," Mrs. Thatcher finished firmly. "Begging your pardon, my lady, but I've known you since you were a girl. You've carried your burdens with grace, but even the strongest shoulders need rest."

Emily's eyes stung with unexpected tears. "Thank

you, Mrs. Thatcher," she said softly. "Your kindness means more than you know."

As the housekeeper bustled away, Emily continued her walk, her thoughts a tumultuous mix of longing and propriety. Mr. Winters was a rogue, yes, but there was a gentleness beneath his rakish exterior that called to her. Still, she had responsibilities—to her son, to her reputation, to the memory of her late husband.

There could be no future with Mr. Winters, she reminded herself. And yet, no matter how often she told herself that, her traitorous heart whispered of possibilities.

Five

The door creaked open as Emily stepped into Nicolas's chamber, a servant carrying a tray laden with steaming broth, hearty stew, freshly baked bread, and a strawberry tart behind her. The comforting aroma of the food mingled with the scents of beeswax and firewood enveloping the room.

Propped against the pillows, his hair neatly combed, Mr. Winters looked better than he had since he'd arrived at Gilford Manor. His eyes, though weary, gleamed with determination, and the flush of fever had left his face.

"I trust you are feeling better this evening?" Emily inquired, offering a gentle smile as she placed her hand on his forehead. "I daresay the fever has broken."

"Indeed. And I must say, your presence alone has been most restorative," he replied, his voice hoarse but still carrying that teasing lilt she had come to recognize. His grin, though weary, held the playful charm of a man who was not entirely helpless, despite appearances.

Emily chuckled softly as she fluffed the pillows behind him, her hand brushing his shoulder as she adjusted the tray. She withdrew quickly, the casual intimacy of the moment startling her, though she did her best to keep her composure.

As she helped Nicolas sit up, he watched her, a look of curiosity flickering in his gaze. He had become dependent on this woman, a stranger who had taken him in, cared for him, and shown him a kindness that went beyond mere duty. He found himself drawn to her quiet strength and compassion, though he could not yet fathom why.

With Nicolas settled, Emily gestured for the servant to reveal the tray. The smell of broth and warm bread made his stomach growl in protest. She laughed softly. Her laughter eased the quiet tension between them, soothing the moment.

"It seems your appetite is well and truly back." Amusement lit her face. "That is certainly a good sign."

Nicolas grinned, his familiar roguish charm

flickering to life. "Under your care, I am feeling quite restored. I daresay, I find myself craving more than just food."

Emily felt her cheeks warm at his boldness, and she turned to arrange the tray over his lap, using the task as a distraction from the quickening of her pulse. The servant curtsied and quietly departed, leaving the two of them alone in the room. The atmosphere grew heavier with the silence, the weight of their shared glances and unspoken words settling like a fine mist over them.

"Well, Mr. Winters," Emily said, her voice breaking the quiet as she attempted to steer the conversation back to safer ground. "I do hope you will find this meal to your liking. Cook has been most attentive."

Amusement softened his features, but there was something deeper there as well—something more earnest than his usual lighthearted charm. "I have no doubt it will be delightful," he said, his tone softer now. "Though, if I may be so bold, it is your company that I truly find nourishing."

"You are incorrigible." She averted her attention to the tray.

Though his words carried their usual teasing tone, there was something different in his gaze. A depth, a gratitude that he hadn't allowed to surface until now. He cleared his throat, his eyes softening as he met her gaze.

She saw a vulnerability in his expression that made her breath catch. It was in that moment she realized how deeply this man affected her. In a short handful of days, their lives had become intertwined by an unexpected twist of fate, and she could not help but feel the stirrings of something unfamiliar, something dangerous and compelling.

She had always prided herself on her self-control, her ability to care without attachment. But with Nicolas, something was different. It was more than compassion—it was the unsettling realization that she wanted to care for him, in a way that went beyond simple human kindness.

He took a tentative bite of the broth, his hand trembling slightly as he lifted the spoon. Emily watched as he swallowed, her heart lifting in quiet triumph at this small victory in his recovery. She allowed herself to admire the powerful lines of his face, the way his jaw tightened as he concentrated on the simple act of eating.

"Is it to your liking, Mr. Winters?" she asked, her voice laced with genuine curiosity.

He nodded, his lips curling into a playful smirk. "It is divine. However, your kindness has done more to restore me than any meal could. For that, I am forever in your debt."

Emily shook her head, her chestnut hair catching the sunlight streaming through the window. "There is no debt to be paid. I only did what any decent person would have done."

But even as she spoke, Emily knew that was not entirely true. She had gone beyond what was expected of her—perhaps far beyond it—and though she told herself it was merely compassion that drove her, there was another feeling growing within her that she did not dare name.

As Nicolas continued to eat, her mind turned back to the letter she had found in his coat pocket. The smudged ink and the urgency of its words had been lingering at the back of her thoughts since she had first read it. She knew it was improper to pry, but her curiosity would not be quelled, and she could no longer justify withholding the note from him.

She reached into her pocket and withdrew the letter, her fingers brushing the folded parchment as she gathered the courage to broach the subject.

"Mr. Winters," she began carefully, "shortly after you were brought here, I discovered this letter in your coat. It is addressed to you and speaks of an urgent matter, though parts of it are damaged."

He set his spoon down, his brow furrowing as he took the letter from her. Their fingers brushed for the briefest moment, sending a jolt through Emily's arm that she was not prepared for. She withdrew her hand quickly, watching as he scanned the contents of the letter, his expression darkening with concern that soon turned to confusion.

"It seems there is trouble brewing at home," he said, half to himself. "A matter I must attend to as soon as I am able, though I fear I am in no condition to travel, and I fear I do not recall what the matter entails."

Emily's heart tightened at the worry etched into his features. She instinctively reached out, her hand resting on his arm in a gesture of reassurance. "Whatever it is, I am certain it can wait until you have recovered. And I will ensure you regain the strength to face it."

Nicolas looked up at her then, his gaze locking onto hers with a gratitude so deep it took her breath away.

The room grew quiet again, the only sound the crackling of the fire in the hearth. The winter sun dipped toward the horizon, casting long shadows and bathing the room in a soft amber glow. Emily sat beside him, her hand still resting lightly on his arm, drawing strength from the steady heat of his skin beneath her fingertips.

For the first time, Nicolas felt a vulnerability that he had not allowed himself to acknowledge since his arrival. Emily's kindness, her unwavering care, had touched something within him, something he had long buried beneath layers of charm and mischief. He had been wrong to think himself undeserving of such tenderness, and as he gazed at the woman beside him, he knew he wanted more from her. If only for a fleeting moment.

"Lady Gilford," he began, his voice quiet but resolute, "I know I am an unrepentant rake, but I find myself without the words to properly express my gratitude. You have shown me a compassion that goes beyond mere duty, and I am truly humbled by it."

The weight of his words enveloped her, their sincerity stirring emotions she had long kept at bay. She had done what she believed to be right, but it was more than that now. It had become personal.

"You owe me nothing, Nicolas," she replied softly, her gaze lowering to where their hands now rested together. "I did what I felt was right." Her cheeks warmed at her boldness.

"All the same, I am forever in your debt, Emily."

His name on her lips filled her with longing, and she swallowed hard.

The silence stretched between them, filled with the unspoken realization that they had crossed a boundary, that something had shifted in the space between them. Emily, suddenly aware of the intimacy of their situation, gently withdrew her hand and smoothed the fabric of her skirts, seeking to regain her composure.

Nicolas, too, sensed the change in the air, though he was not inclined to retreat from it as she had. He cleared his throat, his gaze drifting to the window where the fading sunlight bathed the room in warm hues. "It seems we must both adjust to the rather unusual nature of our acquaintance," he said, a small smile tugging at his lips.

She allowed herself a smile in return, the tension between them easing slightly. "Indeed. Fate, it appears, has a peculiar way of bringing people together."

Nicolas's eyes sparkled with renewed energy as he leaned back against the pillows, his gaze never leaving hers. "You have been far too modest. It is clear to me that you are no ordinary woman, and I find myself wishing to know you better."

She felt her heart skip at his praise, though she knew better than to fall for the flattery of a notorious rogue. "Mr. Winters," she countered, her tone light but firm, "I assure you, I am quite ordinary. Merely a woman who could not, in good conscience, leave a man to suffer alone."

He laughed, the sound low and rich, filling the room with a warmth that made her heart race. "Ah, but that is where you are wrong, dear lady," he said, his voice dropping to a near-whisper. "In a world filled with self-interest, your selflessness stands out like a beacon. You are quite extraordinary."

Her breath hitched, caught off guard by the intensity of his perusal and the sincerity in his words. She had never thought of herself as anything remarkable, but in that moment, under his scrutiny, she wondered if perhaps there was more to her than she had ever allowed herself to believe.

As his words hung in the air, a shift occurred between them. The room, once filled with quiet formality, now pulsed with a new tension, one that neither could name but both felt deep in their bones. His gaze held a depth that spoke of vulnerability, of gratitude, and perhaps something more dangerous.

"I owe you a debt." His hand moved to cover hers where it lay on her lap. His touch was gentle, but it sent a current of warmth through her that she could not ignore. "When you are ready, name your price. I assure you that you will have whatever it is you desire."

Emily's breath caught, her heart pounding as she met his gaze. "You owe me nothing," she whispered, her voice trembling slightly.

His fingers tightened around hers, his gaze searching hers with an intensity that made her feel as though he could see straight into her soul. "You saved my life, and for that, I owe you more than I can ever repay." His gaze lingering on hers. "You have shown me a kindness I did not expect... and one I will not forget."

The air between them thickened. Every breath she took felt more pronounced. His fingers, still resting against hers, were a reminder of just how fragile the line between duty and desire was. Emily had never imagined that caring for this man, a stranger in every sense of the word, would lead to this—a moment of connection so profound it left her breathless.

Six

Two days later, and unwilling to spend another day in bed, Nicolas had insisted on getting dressed and going down to breakfast rather than accepting the tray Willy had brought him. He was eager to dine with Emily as a friend rather than as her patient. A renewed vigor pulsed through him as he navigated the halls.

With a mischievous glint in his gaze, he made his way into the breakfast room. The fire crackled merrily in the hearth as the morning sun washed over the room. The comforting aroma of freshly baked bread and sizzling bacon wafted from the sideboard, making his mouth water.

Emily sat at the table, her chestnut hair falling in soft waves around her face. As he entered, she rose gracefully to her feet, hazel eyes filled with concern.

"Mr. Winters, are you certain you should be out of bed? Please, allow me to assist you." She moved toward him, hands outstretched.

He held up a hand, halting her progress. "I assure you, I am quite recovered. Your excellent care has worked wonders." A flash of amusement passed through his gaze. "In fact, I believe I can manage procuring my own breakfast this morning. I would not want to impose upon your kindness any further."

Her brow furrowed slightly. "It is no imposition, I assure you. You are still recovering."

"And I am deeply grateful for all you have done," Nicolas said, his voice full of gratitude. "But I am eager to resume some semblance of normalcy. I long to be treated as a proper houseguest, rather than an invalid confined to his sickbed."

A flicker of understanding crossed Emily's face. She nodded, her gaze softening. "Very well, Mr. Winters. If you insist on fending for yourself, far be it from me to stand in your way." Her tone was light, teasing even.

A rush of gratitude warmed him as he offered her a smile. He knew his pride demanded that he assert some independence, to prove to himself and to her that he was on the mend. Yet A part of him would miss her gentle ministrations—the soft touch of her hand, the quiet care she offered him with every gesture.

"Shall we break our fast together, then?" Nicolas asked, gesturing toward the table with a plate heaped with eggs, bacon, kippers, and bread in his hands. "I would be delighted to share a meal in your charming company."

Emily inclined her head, a rosy hue coloring her cheeks. "It would be my pleasure, Mr. Winters."

"I prefer it when you call me Nicolas," he said with a teasing arch of his brow. "After all, we are friends."

She smiled. "Indeed we are, Nicolas."

The sound of his name on her lips shot through him, stirring feelings he had not expected. After all, it was not the first time she had spoken it. Why did it affect him so throughly this time? He shook his head, clearing the thought as he moved toward the table.

They took their seats across from one another, the morning sunlight streaming through the windows. He felt a sense of contentment wash over him as he ate.

Their conversation flowed effortlessly as they partook of the delectable spread before them. Nicolas regaled Emily with tales of his mischievous exploits, his gaze sparkling with mirth as he recounted the pranks he and his friends had played over the years. Emily smiled more than she had in years, swept up in the easy banter and warmth of his company.

"I must confess," she said, her smile radiant, "I envy the carefree nature of your youth. Mine was spent in the quiet solitude of my father's library, lost in the pages of countless books or under the stern gaze of my governess."

Nicolas leaned forward, his interest piqued. "And what literary adventures did you embark upon? I imagine you as a young girl, dreaming of far-off lands and daring escapades."

Her voice turned wistful as she said, "Indeed, I traveled the world through those stories, experiencing the joys and sorrows of a thousand different lives. It was a solace, in a way, to lose myself in the written word. One I still very much enjoy."

As the days passed, Nicolas and Emily found themselves drawn into a comfortable routine, their friendship deepening with each shared moment. Mornings were spent in companionable silence, reading or attending to household matters, while afternoons found them engaged in lively discussions or friendly games of cards. And as their friendship grew, so did the spark of attraction that sizzled between them.

One particularly chilly afternoon, as they sat before the roaring fire in the library, Emily glanced up from her needlework to find Nicolas watching her intently. "Is something amiss, Nicolas?" she asked, a playful smile tugging at the corners of her lips.

He chuckled softly, shaking his head. "Not at all. I was merely admiring your skill with a needle. It seems there is no end to your talents."

She ducked her head, a faint blush staining her cheeks. "You flatter me, sir. I fear my talents are quite ordinary compared to those of many ladies in London society."

"Ah, but that is where you are mistaken," Nicolas countered, leaning forward in his chair. "For it is not just your skill that sets you apart, but the grace and kindness with which you wield it."

Four days later, they sat across from one another, engrossed in a game of cards. Emily studied her hand, her brow furrowed in concentration, while Nicolas found himself distracted by the way the sunlight danced upon her chestnut locks.

"I believe it is your turn," Emily said, glancing up at him with a playful smile.

Nicolas startled, realizing he had been staring. "Apologies, Emily. I seem to have lost my focus." He placed a card on the table, his fingers brushing against hers. The fleeting contact sent a shiver down his spine, and he wondered if she felt it too.

As they continued their game, their conversation turned to more personal matters. Emily spoke of her late husband, a kind and gentle man who had left her too soon. Nicolas listened attentively, his heart aching for the sorrow she had endured. In turn, he shared his own hopes and dreams, his desire to make a difference in the world, to leave a legacy beyond his reputation as a charming rogue.

In these moments, the outside world seemed to fall away, leaving only the two of them connected by a bond that grew stronger with each passing day. Nicolas knew he was venturing into uncertain territory, that the emotions stirring within him were as dangerous as they were compelling. Yet as he gazed into Emily's warm hazel eyes, he found himself willing to risk it all for the chance to bask in her presence just a little longer.

Emily placed her last card on the table, a triumphant smile gracing her lips. "It appears I have won this round, Nicolas."

He chuckled. "Indeed, you have. I concede defeat to your superior skills."

As they tidied the cards, their fingers brushed once more, lingering a heartbeat longer than necessary. Emily felt a warmth spreading through her, a longing she found herself sorry tempted to explore. She knew it was improper, that she should guard her heart against such feelings, but in Nicolas's presence, she found herself yearning for something more.

"I must confess," she began, her voice soft and tinged with vulnerability, "that these afternoons spent in your company have brought me a great deal of comfort. Since my husband's passing, I have often felt adrift, longing for the companionship and understanding of another."

Nicolas's gaze softened, his hand instinctively reaching out to cover hers. "I cannot begin to imagine the depth of your loss. But please know that you are not alone. I am here, not only as a friend but as someone who truly sees and appreciates the remarkable woman you are."

Her breath caught in her throat, her eyes glistening with unshed tears. "Thank you, Nicolas. Your words mean more to me than you could possibly know."

They sat in comfortable silence, their hands entwined, as the crackling fire cast a warm glow upon their faces. They became lost in the tender intimacy of shared understanding and unspoken desires.

As the clock chimed, signaling the lateness of the hour, they reluctantly parted, their fingers slipping apart with a final, gentle caress. Emily stood, her heart racing as she met his gaze, the intensity in his eyes mirroring the longing in her own.

"Until tomorrow, Nicolas," she said, her voice soft and filled with promise.

"Until tomorrow, Emily." His words were a vow, a pledge of the unspoken emotions that danced between them.

As she left the room, he watched her go, his heart swelling with a desire he had never known before. The sensation unsettled him, and he released a sigh, dismissing the odd yearning. She was his friend— nothing more.

The following evening, Nicolas found himself once again in the parlor, the warmth of the fire and the gentle rustling of Emily's skirts as she moved about the room, creating a soothing ambiance. As they settled into their now-familiar routine, he could not help but marvel at the ease and comfort that had grown between them.

He wished the snow had never begun to melt, but knew the time for him to leave drew near. Pushing the thoughts away, he focused on Emily.

Her melodic voice filled the room as she read aloud from a book of poetry, the words painting vivid images in Nicolas's mind. Yet, as much as he tried to focus on the verses, his thoughts kept drifting to the reason he had begun this journey in the first place—The memory hit him like a blow to the gut. His sister's impending marriage to Lord Forge.

As if sensing his distraction, Emily paused in her reading, her gaze meeting his with a look of concern. "Is everything alright?"

A shadow passed over Nicolas's face as his thoughts drifted back to the letter, the weight of his sister's predicament settling heavily on him. "I remember," he hesitated, unsure of how much to reveal. "I was on my way to help my sister," he admitted, his brow furrowing. "Now I fear I may have been away too long."

Emily set the book aside, her full attention now on Nicolas. "Have you remembered what happened to you? Do you know how you came to be injured?"

"No, but that missive was regarding my sister. She is to be married to a man I believe to be wholly unsuitable for her." He sighed, running a hand through his hair. "The scoundrel tricked her into a compromising situation and thereby forced her hand. I had hoped to reach London in time to stop the wedding, to save her. But now..."

"I understand your concern," Emily said, her hand reaching out to rest gently on his arm. "But perhaps there is still time. The roads are clearing, and travel will soon be possible again."

At her touch, Nicolas felt a spark of desire course through him, his skin tingling where her fingers lingered. He looked up, his gaze locking with hers, and in that moment, he saw a flicker of something deeper, a longing that mirrored his own.

Emily, as if suddenly aware of the intimacy of her gesture, withdrew her hand, a faint blush coloring her cheeks. She rose from her seat, moving toward the window, her gaze fixed on the world outside.

"The snow is melting fast," she observed, her voice tinged with a mix of relief and sadness. "My son, Mathew, will be home soon." She paused, her next words spoken so softly that Nicolas had to strain to hear them. "And you will be leaving."

Nicolas stood, drawn to her side by an invisible force. He wanted to tell her that leaving was the last thing he desired, that the thought of being parted from her filled him with a deep ache. But the words remained unspoken, caught in his throat as he wrestled with the conflicting emotions that warred within him.

"Emily, I..." he began, his voice rough with emotion. "I think it best if I leave at first light. My horse should have little issue navigating the remaining snow."

She turned to face him, her eyes shadowed. "I will always treasure the friendship we have built." She reached up to cup his cheek, her touch feather-light and filled with tenderness.

"As will I." Nicolas pressed his cheek into her palm.

They stood there, frozen in a moment that seemed to stretch on for eternity, surrounded by the unspoken emotions that hung in the air between them.

His eyes fluttered closed for a moment as he savored the warmth of her palm against his skin. When he opened them again, he found Emily's gaze locked on his, the hazel depths swirling with a myriad of emotions.

Then, as if drawn by an invisible force, he lowered his head, his lips capturing hers in a searing kiss. She melted into his embrace, her arms winding around his neck as she pressed herself closer to his lean, muscular frame. The taste of her, sweet and intoxicating, filled his senses, igniting a fire within him that threatened to consume them both.

He deepened the kiss, savoring the warmth of her lips against his. Her quiet sigh sent a thrill through him, a confirmation of the passion simmering between them.

Her fingers threaded through his dark hair,

tugging gently as she matched his fervor with her own. The heat of her body pressed against his, melting the lingering cold of the winter afternoon and replacing it with a heat that burned bright and steady.

Lost in the passion of the moment, Nicolas allowed his hands to roam over the curves of her body, memorizing every dip and swell through the fabric of her dress. She arched into his touch, her own hands sliding beneath his coat to explore the planes of his back, the sensation sending sparks of desire coursing through his veins.

This is perfect, he thought, lost in the haze of passion. She is perfect.

But even as the words formed in his mind, reality came crashing down around them. The ticking of the clock seemed deafening in the silence between them, a cruel reminder that time, always the enemy, was slipping away. With a reluctant sigh, he broke the kiss, resting his forehead against hers as he struggled to catch his breath.

"We cannot," he whispered, his voice rough with emotion. "As much as I want this, as much as I want you, we both know you deserve better than a few fleeting moments. You deserve more than I have to offer."

She nodded, her heart pounding. "I know." She

traced the line of his jaw with a tenderness that made his heart ache. "But for one perfect moment, I allowed myself to forget who I am."

Nicolas pressed a gentle kiss to her forehead, breathing in the scent of her, committing it to memory. He stepped back, the cold rush of air between them a stark reminder of the reality they faced.

She smoothed her skirts, her gaze downcast as she composed herself, the mask of propriety slipping back into place. "I will arrange for your horse to be ready at first light, Nicolas," she said, her voice steady despite the turmoil he knew she felt. "I wish you a safe journey to London and a successful resolution to your family matters."

Nicolas bowed, the formality of the gesture belying the intimacy they had just shared. "Thank you, Emily," he said, his own voice carefully controlled. "I shall carry the memory of our time together with me always."

With a final, lingering look, he turned and strode from the room, his heart heavy with the weight of all that remained unspoken between them. And as he readied for bed, he could not shake the feeling that he was leaving a piece of himself behind, forever entwined with the woman who had saved him.

Seven

E mily stood at the frosted window, her breath fogging the glass as she gazed out at the frigid night. The winter's chill showed no signs of abating, its fury mirroring the turmoil stirring within her. Her fingers sketched absent patterns on the frosted pane, reflecting the restlessness knotting in her chest.

"What am I to do?" she whispered to herself. The thought of Nicolas, just down the hall, sent a tremor through her that had nothing to do with the chill seeping through the windowpane.

Emily turned from the window, pacing the length of her bedchamber. The soft swish of her nightgown against the rug echoed in the quiet room. Her gaze fell upon her writing desk, where an unfinished letter to her dear friend Beatrice lay forgotten.

Bea would know just what to say. Emily sighed. She could almost hear Beatrice's no-nonsense voice, reminding her she was a woman allowed to have desires. Allowed to live her life.

The wind outside howled, rattling the shutters and strengthening the longing that had taken root in Emily's heart. She hugged herself, rubbing her arms for warmth. For close to a fortnight, the storm had cut them off from the world, leaving her and Nicolas in a bubble of seclusion. But now that the snow had mostly melted, all of that would change. He would leave in the morning and she might never see him again.

Would she regret not having gone to him? Not ceasing the opportunity to feel his body against hers? She longed to feel alive. To have her blood burning with desire. Her body pulsing with need and cresting with satisfaction. It had been years since she'd lain with a man. Years since she had truly felt the thrill of passion.

Would it truly be so wrong to take this one night? To feel truly alive, if only for a fleeting moment? She had given so much of herself to others—to her grief, to charity and duty. Why shouldn't she have this one thing?

What would it hurt to go to Nicolas? To take something for herself? She would wager her friends at the Wicked Widows club would not hesitate if they were in her slippers. The thought caused the corners of her lips to curve up.

"I am a widow, after all," Emily said, her fingers toying with the locket that held her late husband's portrait. "Am I not allowed a bit of indiscretion?" But even as the words left her lips, doubt crept in. The weight of societal expectations pressed down upon her, threatening to smother the tiny flame of hope that had kindled in her breast.

Emily moved to stoke the fire, watching as the flames leapt higher. The warmth caressed her skin, a poor substitute for the touch she truly craved. Her mind wandered to Nicolas—his tousled dark hair, those seductive green eyes that seemed to see right through her, and his roguish grin.

"What would it be like," she wondered aloud, "to feel his hands on my skin?" The words hung in the air, full of possibility and danger.

Her hand hovered over the flame as doubt gnawed at her resolve. What would society say? What would he think of her? Yet, the fire in her blood had awakened something long dormant, a yearning she could scarcely ignore.

Emily felt as though she stood on the precipice of something monumental, teetering between propriety and passion. Her heart raced with the thrill of it all, even as her mind cautioned restraint.

She moved back to the window, pressing her palm flat against the glass. The cold seeped into her skin, grounding her in the present moment. Outside, the world was dark and windswept, the familiar landscape transformed into something wild and untamed. Emily felt a kinship with that wildness, a part of herself longing to break free from the constraints that had bound her for so long.

Her fingers curled against the glass, her resolve crystallizing with each passing moment. The quiet ticking of the mantel clock seemed to echo her quickening heartbeat. She took a deep breath.

"To the devil with it," she said, her voice barely audible above the howling wind. "I have mourned. I have been proper. But I am still alive, and I deserve..." She trailed off, the word 'passion' caught in her throat.

With trembling hands, Emily reached for the candle on her bedside table. Its warm glow cast dancing shadows on the walls as she moved toward her bedroom door. She paused, her hand on the doorknob, as doubt crept in.

If anyone should find out, she thought, biting her lower lip. But then, how would they? The isolation of the storm seemed to cocoon her, offering a strange kind of freedom. No-one was here other than her servants and they were all abed. They would never gossip about her at any rate.

Emily stepped into the darkened hallway, her bare feet silent on the plush carpet. The flickering candlelight illuminating her path.

As she approached Nicolas's room, her heart thundered against her ribs. She could hear his playful voice in her mind, teasing her about her boldness. The thought brought a small smile to her lips, despite her nervousness.

She notched her chin, her confidence growing. She was taking control of her own happiness. Surely, there could be no shame in that? With each step, she felt both exhilarated and terrified.

She paused outside Nicolas's door, her hand hovering over the handle, her breath coming in short, quick gasps. The memory of Nicolas's smoldering gaze teased her thoughts, as if beckoning her. Could she really do this?

Taking a deep breath, she grasped the door handle, the cold metal a stark contrast to her flushed skin. Her heart pounded with anticipation as she prepared to step into his room and, if she had her way, his bed.

As she turned the handle, desire coiled low in her belly, an ache that demanded to be sated. For too long, she had ignored her own wants and needs out of a sense of propriety and grief. But in the days since his arrival, something had awakened inside her —a yearning to feel again, to embrace passion and pleasure. And she instinctively knew Nicolas, with his roguish charm and heated glances, was the only man who could satisfy her.

Emily pushed the door open, slipping inside the dimly lit bedchamber. The click of the latch vibrated through her. There would be no turning back now.

Nicolas stood by the window, his broad shoulders silhouetted by moonlight filtering through the pane. At the sound of her entrance, he turned, eyes darkening as he took in the sight of her—chestnut hair tumbling loose around her shoulders, the thin white fabric of her nightgown doing little to conceal her womanly curves.

"Emily?" His rich baritone sent a shiver down her spine. "What are you doing here at this hour? Are you alright? Has something happened?"

She stepped closer, pulse pounding in her throat. The way he looked at her, gaze darkening with unmistakable desire, emboldened her. "I could not sleep for wanting you."

His lips parted on a sharp inhale. "Emily—"

"I am a grown woman and a widow besides," she said, tilting her chin. The thrill of defiance emboldening her. "I can no longer ignore what I feel for you… this attraction between us."

Closing the remaining distance between them, she placed a trembling hand on his chest, feeling the drum of his heartbeat through the fine linen of his shirt. "I know you want me too, Nicolas. I see it in your eyes."

He captured her hand in his larger one, strong fingers caressing her palm and sending sparks skittering over her flesh. "More than you can possibly imagine."

"Then show me," she breathed.

Eight

⌒⌒

N icolas's breath ghosted over her lips as he paused, searching her gaze. "Are you sure, Emily?"

She nodded, her pulse hammering in her throat. "Yes. I have never been more certain."

With a low groan, Nicolas pulled her close, capturing her lips in a kiss so searing it stole the very breath from her. Emily wrapped her arms around his neck, her body melding against his, feeling every ridge of muscle beneath his skin.

His powerful hands roamed over her back, igniting trails of fire even through the thin fabric of her nightgown. She arched into his touch, a breathy moan escaping her as his lips trailed scorching kisses along the column of her throat.

Tangling her fingers in his dark hair, she tilted

her head to grant him better access, reveling in the rasp of his evening stubble against her sensitive skin. Each brush of his mouth stoked the flames of her desire higher.

"Nicolas," she gasped as he nipped at her racing pulse. "Please..."

He gentled his attentions, breath hot against her ear as he asked, "Are you certain? Another taste of you and there will be no turning back. I am a rogue, after all."

She drew back enough to frame his face between her palms, her gaze locking with his. "I have never been more certain of anything in my life. I want you. All of you."

Something fierce and primitive flashed in his gaze, as if her declaration had unleashed the passion he'd been holding back. "Then you shall have me. In every way a man can worship a woman."

Lowering his head, Nicolas claimed her lips in a kiss that seared her to her very soul. Emily matched him with equal hunger, bold now in her need. She nipped at his bottom lip, swallowing his answering groan.

Large hands smoothed down her sides to her hips, spanning her waist. He gathered the fabric of her nightgown, inching it higher as he walked her backwards toward the large four-poster bed dominating the room. The backs of her thighs hit the mattress, and she tumbled down onto the counterpane, Nicolas following her without breaking their kiss.

Her pulse thrummed as his solid weight settled over her, the hard ridge of his manhood an insistent press against her belly. Liquid heat pooled low in her abdomen, anticipation burning through her veins. She yearned for his touch on her bare skin, to feel him against her with no barriers between them...

She reached between their bodies, fingers fumbling with the tie of her nightgown. Nicolas drew back just enough to watch, his eyes blazing with passion as the delicate fabric parted. With a shaky exhale, she slipped first one creamy shoulder free, then the other.

His gaze tracked the slow descent of silk, his lips parting on a sharp inhale as she bared her breasts to him. "Beautiful," he breathed, reverence and raw need mingling in that single word.

Unabashedly, she arched up to shimmy the nightgown over her hips and down her legs. The cool air kissed her flushed skin as she lay back against the pillows, clad only in the firelight and Nicolas's heated approval.

"Touch me," she whispered, emboldened by the

stark desire etched across his handsome face. "Everywhere."

He extended one hand, trailing a single finger along her collarbone and down between the valley of her breasts. Goosebumps followed his touch, her nipples hardening as he circled first one, then the other.

"Like this?" he teased, rolling the tight bud between his fingers. Sparks of pleasure streaked straight to her core.

"Yes," she gasped, clutching at his shoulders. He palmed the soft weight of her breast, kneading the flesh as he lowered his head to lave attention on its neglected twin. She keened as his tongue flicked across the sensitized tip, pleasure bordering on pain. "Oh God, Nicolas..."

He pulled the aching point into his mouth and suckled gently, the wet heat shredding the last of her inhibitions. She threaded her fingers through his hair to hold him to her, reveling in each draw of his lips, each scrape of his teeth.

When he switched to her other breast, she was lost, reduced to wordless cries and breathy pleas. Her nails scored his scalp as he tormented first one nipple, then the other, until her hips were rocking frantically against him, seeking fulfillment only he could provide...

Nicolas released her breast with a soft pop, his eyes dark with desire as he lifted his head to capture her lips in a searing kiss. Emily moaned into his mouth, the taste of him mingling with the scent of their arousal. His tongue swept inside to dance with hers, stoking the flames that burned within her core.

Large hands skimmed down her sides to grip her hips, pulling her flush against the hard planes of his body. She could feel the evidence of his want pressing insistently against her, and a thrill raced through her at the knowledge that she affected him so profoundly.

"I want you," Nicolas rasped against her lips, his voice rough with need. "I have wanted you for so long, Emily. From the first moment I saw you."

"Then take me," she breathed. "Take all of me."

With a growl, he claimed her mouth once more, the kiss fierce and demanding. His hands roamed her body, mapping every curve and hollow, each touch branding her very soul. She surrendered to the sensations, lost in a haze of desire as he stoked and kissed her burning flesh.

Nicolas's lips blazed a trail of fire down her neck, across her collarbone, lower still, to the peaked tips of her breasts. He paused there, licking and suckling until she was writhing beneath him.

"More," Emily keened, arching her back in a silent plea. "I need more."

He answered with a flick of his tongue against the sensitive bud, wringing a cry from her lips. Lower he trailed, painting a path down her quivering abdomen with openmouthed kisses. When he reached the thatch of curls at the apex of her thighs, Emily went still, hardly daring to breathe.

Slowly, reverently, Nicolas parted her folds, baring her most intimate flesh to his heated gaze. She threw her head back in anticipation of his touch. Her fingers twisted in the sheets as he brought his tongue to her most intimate place.

Her world narrowed to the exquisite sensations he was drawing from her body. His clever tongue danced over her sensitive flesh, teasing and tasting with expert precision. She clutched at the bedsheets, her back arching as waves of pleasure coursed through her.

"Nicolas," she gasped, her voice barely recognizable to her own ears. "Oh, Nic…"

He groaned against her flesh, the vibrations sending shockwaves of bliss through her core. His hands gripped her thighs, holding her open to his ministrations as he laved and suckled at her sensitive bud. Her breath came in short, sharp pants, her chest heaving as she climbed higher and higher.

"Nicolas," she moaned, one hand leaving the sheets to tangle in his dark hair. "Oh, God... please..."

He hummed against her, the vibrations sending shockwaves of bliss straight to her core. One large hand splayed across her stomach, holding her in place as he continued his sensual assault. The other crept up to cup her breast, fingers plucking at the taut peak.

Emily felt herself climbing higher and higher, chasing a peak she'd nearly forgotten existed. It had been so long since she had felt anything close to this level of passion. Her hips rolled against his mouth of their own accord, seeking more of the delicious friction.

Just as she teetered on the brink, he slipped a finger inside her, curling it in a motion that had her seeing stars. The dual stimulation proved too much. With a husky cry, Emily shattered, waves of ecstasy washing over her in relentless waves.

As she came down from her high, Nicolas placed gentle kisses on her inner thighs, soothing her quivering flesh. He crawled back up her body, capturing her lips in a deep, passionate kiss. The taste of herself on his lips sent a renewed spark of arousal through her still-trembling body and she pressed her hips against him, greedy for more.

"You are exquisite," Nicolas murmured.

"That was..." she breathed against his mouth.

"Only the beginning," he promised, his voice a low rumble that sent shivers down her spine.

Her hands roamed over Nicolas's broad shoulders, relishing the feel of taut muscle beneath her fingertips. A surge of boldness overcame her as she tugged at his shirt, eager to feel his bare skin against hers.

"Off." She tugged at his shirt, breathlessly. "I want to see you."

He chuckled, a low, sensual sound that sent heat pooling low in her belly. "As my lady commands." He sat back on his heels and pulled the garment over his head.

Her breath caught in her throat as she drank in the sight of his bare torso. Lean muscle rippled beneath bronzed skin, a dusting of dark hair trailing tantalizingly down his abdomen. Her fingers itched to trace every dip and plane, to learn the textures of his body as intimately as he had learned hers.

"Do I meet with your approval?" He asked, a hint of teasing in his voice.

In answer, she reached out, running her hands over his chest and down his stomach. She delighted in the way his muscles jumped beneath her touch, in the sharp intake of breath as her fingers dipped below the waistband of his breeches.

"Very much," she whispered, meeting his gaze. The hunger she saw there made her breath catch.

Nicolas caught her wrist, bringing her hand to his lips. He pressed a kiss to her palm, then each fingertip in turn. "You are playing with fire, my dear."

"I do hope to get incinerated." She pulling him down, her mouth finding his in a demanding kiss.

Nicolas growled low in his throat as he claimed her mouth, his kiss fierce and demanding. She matched his passion, her hands roaming over the planes of his back, nails scraping lightly against his skin. She reveled in the way he shuddered against her, in the evidence of his desire pressing insistently against her.

With fumbling fingers, she reached between them to unfasten his breeches. Nicolas broke the kiss, his breath coming in harsh pants as he helped her push the garment down and off. When he settled back over her, she gasped at the feel of his bare skin against hers, the heat of him searing her to her very soul.

"Emily," he said, his voice rough with need. "Are you certain?"

She met his gaze, seeing the mix of desire and concern reflecting back at her. "More certain than I have ever been," she breathed. "I want you inside of me, Nicolas. I crave you."

A groan tore from his throat as he captured her lips once more. His hand slid down her body, fingers dancing over her heated flesh until he reached the apex of her thighs. Her hips bucked as he stroked her, finding her still slick and ready from his earlier attentions.

"Fill me," she gasped against his mouth as she pressed her hips toward him.

Nicolas positioned himself at her entrance, his manhood pressing against her core. Slowly, exquisitely, he eased inside her, his gaze locked with hers. Emily's lips parted on a soft gasp as he entered her, stretching and completing her in ways she had nearly forgotten existed.

She rocked her hips greedily, desperate to feel him move.

He groaned, his forehead pressed against hers as he fought for control. "Easy, love. Let me savor you."

She whimpered, her body ablaze with need. Every nerve ending singing with pleasure. When Nicolas finally moved, she thought she might combust from the sheer ecstasy of it.

He set a languid pace at first, each deep thrust stoking the fire within her. Emily met him movement for movement, her legs wrapping around his waist to draw him closer. Her hands roamed over the planes of his back, feeling the flex and play of muscle beneath her fingertips.

"Oh," she gasped, arching into him. "Nicolas… Please."

He answered her plea by increasing his tempo, driving into her with passionate intensity. The room filled with the sounds of their lovemaking—skin against skin, breathless moans, and whispered endearments.

Emily felt her desire build higher and higher as she chased that elusive peak. He slipped a hand between their bodies, his clever fingers finding that sensitive bundle of nerves. She cried out at the added stimulation, her body trembling on the precipice.

"Let go," he urged, his voice rough with passion. "Come apart for me."

His words were her undoing. With his name on her lips, Emily came apart, her release slamming into her. He followed her over the edge moments later, her name a reverent prayer on his lips.

The fire crackled softly in the hearth, casting a warm glow over their entwined limbs as she traced idle patterns on his chest, marveling at the steady thrum of his heartbeat beneath her fingertips.

"That was..." she began, trailing off as words failed her.

He chuckled, the sound rumbling through his chest. "Indeed, it was." He pressed a kiss to her temple. "You are full of surprises, my lady."

She lifted her head to meet his gaze. "I will have you know, sir, that proper ladies can be quite scandalous when the mood strikes."

"Oh?" His eyebrow arched in amusement. "And does the mood strike you often?"

"Perhaps more often than I care to admit when there is a handsome rake beneath my roof," she replied, her cheeks flushing at her own boldness.

Nicolas's arms tightened around her, drawing her closer. "Then I count myself fortunate to be the recipient of your scandalous attentions."

Her heart swelled at his words, even as a flicker of uncertainty crept in. What would happen when morning came? When he was gone and reality intruded on their passionate interlude?

As if sensing her thoughts, Nicolas tilted her chin up, his gaze searching hers. "What troubles you?"

She bit her lip and shook her head. "Nothing," she lied, not wanting to ruin the time she had with him. Emily settled her head against his chest, allowing herself to soak in the afterglow of what they had shared.

As the night wore on, Emily and Nicolas lay entwined in each other's arms, their breaths mingled in the dimly lit bedroom. Contented smiles danced on their lips as they exchanged soft, lingering kisses and lighthearted banter.

Nicolas rubbed soothing circles on Emily's back, his own gaze glowing with intensity in the firelight. "My darling Emily," he said, his voice husky with emotion. "You have bewitched me entirely."

She traced her fingers along the contours of his face, memorizing every detail. "And you have awakened something in me I thought long dead."

Their bodies moved in perfect synchronicity, each touch igniting new sparks of pleasure. Emily marveled at how Nicolas anticipated her every desire, his hands and lips finding all the right places to make her gasp and shiver.

And as the heat between them built, she lost all sense of time and place. There was only Nicolas, only this night of pure, unbridled passion.

They made love again. Their movements a perfect blend of gentle caresses and passionate embraces. Emily felt herself being swept away by the tide of emotions, each wave bringing her closer to Nicolas in ways she had never believed possible.

As they reached the pinnacle of their pleasure, she clung to him, her body trembling with ecstasy.

She gazed into his passion-filled eyes, finding herself lost in their depths.

"Nicolas," she gasped, her voice barely above a whisper.

He held her close, his lean, athletic body pressed against hers. "Emily," he breathed, his usual playful tone replaced by one of reverence.

For a moment, they remained frozen, savoring the intense wave of bliss that washed over them. Her heart raced, and she could feel his beating just as rapidly against her chest as their breaths filled the room.

Emily soon found herself nestled in Nicolas's arms. The warmth of the fire caressing her skin, casting a soft glow across the room as they settled into a peaceful slumber.

As the first rays of dawn peeked through the curtains, Emily stirred, a contented smile playing on her lips as the memories of the previous night flooded her senses. She stretched languidly, reaching for the warmth beside her, but the space was cold. Empty. She sat up, the memory of their shared passion crashing down on her as she scanned the room, finding no trace of him.

"Nicolas?" She called out, her heart racing as she sat up, clutching the blanket to her chest. The room remained silent, save for the faint crackling of the dying embers in the fireplace.

As reality settled in, her gaze fell upon a folded piece of paper on the nightstand. With trembling fingers, she reached for it, her mind a whirl of emotions.

Dearest Emily,

Forgive me for leaving so suddenly, but I believe it was for the best—for both of us.

Yours, Nicolas

Her heart sunk as she read and reread the words he had written. "Best for who?" she seethed, running her fingers over the ink. He was a rogue after all, to leave without a word. But a coward, too? That was harder to swallow—and after what they had shared.

She closed her eyes, inhaling deeply as she tried to make sense of her conflicting emotions. The joy of their intimate encounter still lingered, yet it was now tinged with heartache. Had she been too forward? Too eager? Or was this simply another of his impulsive acts? She crumbled the letter in her hand.

As she rose from the bed, wrapping herself in her discarded nightgown, she could not help but feel a mix of heartache and anger. Nicolas had stirred feelings in her she thought long buried, and while he had not declared his love for her, his hasty departure stung.

She had given him her heart—her body, and now he was gone. Was she just another conquest to him, another fleeting moment in a rogue's life?

Had she meant nothing to him?

Emily's thoughts whirled as she fled the room, desperate to leave the memories of the prior night behind.

Nine

The carriage rattled over the cobblestones. The scent of coal smoke and horses hung heavy in the air, a stark contrast to the crisp country breeze Nicolas had left behind. With each turn of the wheels, Emily's face flashed before him—her sparkling eyes, her gentle smile. A sharp pang of regret knotted in his chest.

She had haunted him from the moment he rode away from her estate three days past. He arrived at his bachelor flat late last night, then attempted to drink himself into a deep slumber, only to dream of her.

He should not have left her. Running a hand through his hair, he cursed himself. Not without so much as a goodbye. Emily deserved better. But he did not have time for regrets now. Not when Joslyn needed him.

Nicolas barely waited for the carriage to stop when it pulled up in front of his family's townhouse before leaping out, his long legs carrying him swiftly to the door. He raised the brass knocker, his heart pounding with anticipation and worry.

The door swung open, and a blur of auburn hair and cream silk rushed toward him.

"Nicolas," Joslyn cried, flinging herself into his arms. "Oh, thank heavens you are here. I was so worried."

He embraced his sister, feeling her trembling against him. "Joslyn, my dear," he said, his voice soft with concern. "What has happened? Your letter was so vague. Tell me you have not agreed to Forge's proposal."

"I most certainly have not." She pulled back, her eyes shimmering with tears. "It was a dreadful mess, Nicolas. I have been such a fool." She gripped his arms, her slender fingers digging into the fabric of his coat. "But where have you been? I expected you days ago."

A flash of guilt crossed his face. "I was delayed south of Luton. There was a terrible storm." Emily and the time they had spent together flashed through his mind. "Forgive me, Jos. I came as quickly as I could."

Joslyn's brow furrowed. "Luton? It is scarcely a town at all. What on earth were you doing there? I thought you were at Lord Blackwood's estate?"

Nicolas hesitated, torn between confiding in his sister and focusing on her predicament. "It is... a very long story," he said, managing a wry smile. "One best saved for another time. For now, tell me what has happened to you."

As Joslyn spoke, Nicolas guided her into the house. The warm air greeted them, scented with beeswax and lavender, a familiar comfort. He closed the door, shutting out the world beyond. Yet even as he listened to his sister's words, his mind could not help but wander back to Emily, wondering if he had made the right choice in leaving her like he had.

As Joslyn opened her mouth to respond, the sound of approaching footsteps echoed through the marble-floored entry hall. Nicolas turned, his heart swelling with warmth as he saw his parents enter.

"Mother, Father." A genuine smile spread across his face at the sight of them.

Lady Quinton rushed forward, her silk skirts rustling as she enveloped Nicolas in a tight embrace. "My darling boy." She held him close, her voice thick with emotion. "How we have missed you."

Nicolas returned the embrace, taking comfort in the familiar scent of rose water that always clung to his mother's clothes. "And I you, Mother."

As they parted, the Earl of Quinton approached, clasping Nicolas's shoulder with a firm hand. "Welcome home, son," he said, his deep voice resonating with affection.

Nicolas inclined his head. "Thank you, Father. It is good to be back."

The earl grinned, his gaze dancing. "I trust your journey was pleasant? Though I daresay something unpleasant must have happened to delay you."

"A blizzard. And a tumble from my mount. I was injured and became sick, but I assure you I am fully recovered from the ordeal."

"How terrible," Mother said, her hand going to her bosom.

"Oh Nicolas," Joslyn said, resting her hand on his arm. "What you must have endured. And to think it could have been avoided if only I had made better choices."

"Do not fret, Jos. A kind lady took me in and saw me well."

"I should like to thank her," Mother said, moving to stand beside Father.

"Indeed, we shall," Father said, meeting Nicolas's gaze. "What was the lady's name, son?"

Nicolas's breath caught, a sudden rush of memories flooding back, tightening his chest with both longing and guilt. He struggled to maintain his composure, acutely aware of his family's curious gazes upon him.

"Lady Emily Fairchild," he managed, striving for nonchalance. "She was... most kind during my stay."

"We are acquainted with Lady Fairchild." The earl nodded with approval. "I am not surprised she aided you. She has quite a reputation for her caring nature. A credit to her family, that one."

Nicolas nodded, though his mind was far from the conversation. He swallowed hard against the memories of Emily's gentle smile and warm gaze flooding his mind. The ache in his chest, which had momentarily subsided in the joy of reuniting with his family, returned with renewed force.

"Indeed," he murmured, his voice barely above a whisper. "She is... quite remarkable."

As his family continued to chat around him, he found himself lost in thoughts of Emily. The longing to see her again, to hear her laugh and feel the soft touch of her hand, was almost overwhelming. He had never felt like this before—never regretted leaving. Never formed attachments to the women he spent time with. What the devil was wrong with him?

With effort, he dragged his attention back to the present, forcing a smile as he turned to his sister. "Enough about me. Now, Joslyn," he said, his voice steadier than he felt, "tell me everything."

"I shall, but first let us move to the parlor so that we might be more comfortable."

Mother nodded her approval. "I will have tea and biscuits brought in."

A few minutes later, Nicolas settled into a wing-back chair. He leaned forward, elbows on his knees, his gaze fixed on Joslyn.

"What exactly happened with Lord Forge?" he asked, his voice low and tinged with concern. "I need to know every detail."

Joslyn sank into the settee across from him, her slender fingers twisting nervously in her lap. She took a deep breath, her gaze meeting his with a mix of embarrassment and distress.

"Oh, Nic," she began, her voice trembling. "I was such a fool. Lord Forge... he invited me to view his art collection. I thought nothing of it—he had been so charming, so attentive... and you know how I adore art."

Nicolas felt his jaw clench, but he remained silent, allowing his sister to continue.

"When I arrived, he led me to a secluded room. Before I knew what was happening, he... he pulled me close and kissed me." Her cheeks flushed with the memory. "And then, as if on cue, his valet burst in, feigning shock at the scene. He caused such a commotion that others came running, arriving in time to see me wrapped in his arms."

"That scoundrel," Nicolas exclaimed, leaping to his feet. His hands clenched into fists at his sides, his body thrumming with anger. "He planned it. To compromise you and force a marriage. It is no secret he needs a dowery, and yours is substantial."

Joslyn nodded miserably. "I realized it too late. He smiled at me then, Nicolas. It was... it was chilling. He said he would marry me at once to save me from ruin."

Nicolas paced the room, his mind racing. How dare that cur take advantage of his sweet sister? The urge to protect Joslyn, to defend her honor, surged through him like a tidal wave.

"I will kill him," he seethed, danger flashing in his eye. "I will challenge him to a duel. That way, I can look him in the eye as I run him through."

"Nicolas, no." Joslyn took hold of his arm. "You cannot. It is too dangerous and all together unnecessary. What if—"

But Nicolas was beyond reason. His protective instincts, honed by years of looking after Joslyn, had taken over. He gently removed her hand from his arm, his voice softening as he addressed her.

"Do not worry, Jos. He will not get away with this. I swear it." His fists clenched at his sides, rage simmering beneath the surface. He would make Forge pay, no matter the cost. "And you will not be marring him," Nicolas growled the last words.

As he studied his sister's worried face, he could not help but think of Emily. What would she say if she could see him now, ready to risk everything in a duel? The thought gave him pause, but only for a moment. Some things were worth fighting for, and his sister's honor was certainly one of them.

Joslyn's eyes widened, a mix of alarm and determination flashing across her face. She stepped in front of him, blocking his path to the door.

"Nicolas, wait," she called after him, her voice trembling with urgency. "There is something else you must know."

He halted, his brow furrowing. "What is it?"

She took a deep breath, her slender fingers fidgeting with the lace at her wrists. "I... I have already taken matters into my own hands. You see, I am married now. To the Duke of Langley."

Mother reached out and patted Nicolas's hand. "See dear, all is well." She turned toward the door.

"And look, here is our tea. Do sit, and cease this talk of duels."

"Indeed, your sister is Duchess Langley, now." Father beamed at her before returning his attention to Nicolas. "No lasting harm has been done."

Nicolas blinked, his mouth falling open in shock. "Married? To Rafe? But how... when?"

"It happened rather quickly," Joslyn said, her cheeks flushing. "Rafe learned of Lord Forge's scheme and offered to help. We married three days ago, in a private ceremony."

Nicolas's mind reeled. Relief surged through him, followed by gratitude—an unexpected reprieve from the chaos. His sister was safe, her future secured. He sank into a nearby chair, running a hand through his tousled hair. He had questions—lots of questions— but they could wait for now.

"Good God, Jos." He shook his head. "You have certainly been busy while I've been away."

A small smile tugged at her lips. "I could not wait for you to rescue me this time, dear brother. I had to act quickly."

He nodded, his heart swelling with pride and affection for his clever sister. "And Rafe? He truly did this to protect you?"

"He did," Joslyn confirmed, her lips curving into a

soft smile. "He is a true friend, and now, a devoted husband."

Nicolas stood, embracing his sister tightly. "Then I owe him a great debt of gratitude. Where is he now? I must thank him properly for safeguarding you when I could not."

Lady Quinton watched her son as the conversation about Joslyn's marriage wound down. She noted the slight slump of his shoulders, the faraway look in his gaze. Something was amiss with her youngest, and she was determined to uncover it.

"Nicolas, darling." She moved to sit beside him on the chaise. "While we are all overjoyed about Joslyn's fortunate match, I cannot help but notice you seem... distracted. Is something the matter?"

Nicolas startled, his fingers drumming an uneven rhythm on his thigh. He swallowed hard, his gaze darting around the room before settling on his mother's concerned face. The weight of his emotions, held in check for so long, suddenly felt unbearable.

"I..." he began, his voice low and laced with sorrow. He cleared his throat and tried again. "Mother, I fear I have made a terrible mistake."

Mother placed a comforting hand on his arm. "What is it, my dear?"

He closed his eyes, Emily's face swimming before

him. Her warm gaze, the gentle curve of her smile, the way her chestnut hair caught the sunlight, and his heart clenched painfully.

"I think I have fallen in love." The words spilled out before he could stop them, as if saying them made the feeling all the more real. "With Lady Emily Fairchild. And I left her behind, thinking... oh, I do not know what I was thinking." He blew out a frustrated breath. "I did not even say goodbye."

A collective gasp echoed through the room, and Nicolas opened his eyes to find his family staring at him in varying degrees of surprise and delight.

"Nicolas, that is wonderful news." Joslyn clapped her hands together. "Except for the part about leaving with such haste. But I am certain she will forgive you."

Father chuckled. "Well, well. It seems our boy has finally been tamed. And by such a wonderful lady. She will be a credit to our family as well."

Nicolas swallowed, the weight of his family's expectations settling over him. Could he be the man Emily deserved? He exhaled a slow breath.

"I fear you have gotten ahead of yourselves." Nicolas shook his head, a rueful smile playing at his lips. "Tamed? Hardly. But changed, certainly. Emily... she is unlike anyone I have ever known. Her kindness, her strength, her ability to find joy even in the face of adversity... she is remarkable."

Mother squeezed his hand. "Oh, my darling boy. I can see how deeply you care for her. Yet you look so forlorn. Surely this is cause for celebration?"

Nicolas sighed, running a hand through his hair. "I fear I may have ruined everything when I left her as I did, and now... well, I am uncertain she will have me."

"Nonsense," his father interjected, his voice firm but kind. "Lady Fairchild is every bit as remarkable as you say. She will understand your haste to aid your sister. And if she truly returns your feelings, she will welcome you back with open arms."

Joslyn nodded enthusiastically. "Father's right, Nic. You must not lose hope. Tell us more about your time with her—I want to know everything about how she captured my brother's elusive heart."

As he spoke of Emily—her kindness, her spirit— he realized how deeply she had burrowed into his heart. How every small thing she did had slowly unraveled the man he had been, leaving him bare before her.

He described her charitable works and her gentle spirit, the way she cared for him and befriended him, and he felt a weight lift from his shoulders. The love and support of his family surrounded him, buoying his spirits and kindling his hope for a future with Emily by his side.

A future he had not even known he'd wanted until now. He was a bloody halfwit, to be sure—a rake who most defiantly did not deserve Emily, but one who was selfish enough to pursue her despite it.

Nicolas paced the length of the parlor, his fingers tracing the spine of a book he'd plucked from the shelf. The warmth of the crackling fire did little to quell the restlessness in his heart.

"I cannot stop thinking about her," he confessed, his voice barely above a whisper. "Every moment we spent together, every laugh we shared... it is all etched in my memory."

His mother leaned forward, her gaze soft with understanding. "What is it about Emily that captivates you so?"

He paused, a wistful smile playing at his lips. "It is the way she sees the world, Mother. Despite the hardships she has faced, there is a light in her that refuses to dim. When she speaks of her charitable works, her eyes shine with such passion..."

"You truly are in love," Joslyn said, her voice tinged with excitement. "But brother, what do you intend to do now?"

Nicolas's grip tightened on the book, his knuckles whitening. "I must return to her. I have been a fool. If there is any chance she might forgive me…" His voice faltered, but his resolve hardened. He had to try. "I must fight for her. For my chance at happiness."

His father nodded with approval. "That's the spirit, my boy. A love like this is worth fighting for."

"I had hoped to keep you here for Christmas," Mother said. "Your brother is due home in two days' time and I was so looking forward to spending the holiday with all of my children. But there is not time to spare. You must go to Lady Fairchild at once."

As the family continued to discuss his plans, Nicolas could almost see Emily, standing in the parlor of her country estate, the soft winter sunlight streaming through the leaded-glass windows and catching in her hair. The thought of holding her again, of confessing his true feelings, sent a thrill of anticipation through him.

"I will leave for Luton at first light," he said, his decision crystallizing. "I only hope I am not too late." The thought of never holding her again, of never making things right, clawed at his chest.

The path ahead was uncertain, but he knew with an unwavering conviction that Emily was worth any risk.

Ten

"Oh, drat," Mathew said, frustration creasing his brow as the delicate ivory sticks tumbled onto the table.

Emily could not help but chuckle at her son's frustration. "Patience, dearest. Spillikins is all about a steady hand and a calm heart."

She leaned forward, her gaze warm with affection as she demonstrated the proper technique. "Watch closely. See how gently it is done."

Mathew watched, his face a mirror of concentration. A triumphant grin spread across Emily's features as she extracted a stick without disturbing the others. "Your turn," she said.

As Mathew's hands moved toward the pile, Emily's thoughts wandered, unbidden, to another set of hands—larger, stronger, yet equally gentle. She shook her head, forcing the image of Nicolas from her mind.

A sennight had passed since that fateful morning when she awoke to find him gone, his presence fading like the last traces of moonlight giving way to the morning sun. The ache in her chest threatened to overwhelm her, but Emily steeled herself against it.

"Well done, Mathew." Emily forced a bright smile, pushing aside her sorrow. "You are improving rapidly."

"Do you think I will best Freddie Harrington when we return to Eton?" he asked.

Emily smiled, though it did not quite reach her eyes. "With practice, I believe you will."

As Mathew set up for another round, her gaze drifted to the frost-etched windowpane. The winter landscape beyond seemed to mock her with its serene beauty, so at odds with the tumult in her heart.

The memory of Nicolas's warmth beside her, his whispered endearments, the feeling of completeness she had experienced in his arms—it all came rushing back with painful clarity. How could he have left without a word? Without an explanation?

Her hand trembled as she reached for an ivory stick. She had to be strong, for Mathew, for herself.

She could not allow herself to be consumed by thoughts of a man who had so callously abandoned her.

"Steady, Mother," Mathew reminded her.

Taking a deep breath, Emily squared her shoulders. "Indeed." She smiled at her son. And as she slipped the stick free, she silently vowed to move forward. She would find happiness again—with or without Nicolas Winters. Yet, even as she made this promise to herself, she could not quite quell the traitorous hope that still flickered in her heart.

Nonsense. Nicolas had made his choice when he left without a word. Now she had to accept that there was no future for them. She could not allow hope to prolong her pain.

A sharp knock at the door startled Emily from her thoughts. Mathew jumped up, eager to answer it in the butler's absence. Emily placed a gentle, steadying hand on his shoulder, her thoughts briefly slipping away.

"Allow me, darling," she said, smoothing her skirts as she rose.

As she approached the door, the sound of familiar laughter drifted through, bringing an involuntary smile to her face. Emily opened the door to the sight of her dearest friends, Lady Charlotte Ashbourne and Miss Beatrice Sinclair, their arms full of parcels, cheeks aglow with the crisp winter air.

"Merry Christmas," Charlotte said, enveloping Emily in a warm embrace that smelled of cinnamon and evergreen.

Beatrice, ever the pragmatist, raised an eyebrow. "Are you going to leave us freezing on your doorstep all day, Em?"

Emily chuckled, stepping aside to usher them in. "Heaven forbid. Come in, come in."

As her friends bustled into the parlor, shedding cloaks and gloves, Emily felt a weight lift from her shoulders. Their presence brought a lightness she sorely needed.

"We have brought treats," Charlotte announced, presenting a basket of freshly baked scones.

"I will take those," Mathew said, reaching out for the basket. "I am famished."

Charlotte laughed, handing him the goodies. "Do take care not to eat them all at once."

Beatrice snorted, her attention turning to Emily as Mathew strode away with his treasure. "And something a touch stronger for after Mathew is abed." She produced a bottle of fine brandy with a wink.

Emily's eyes widened. "Beatrice. You should not have."

"Oh, but I should," Beatrice replied, her gaze twinkling with mischief. "After all, what are friends for if not to provide a good time?"

As they settled by the fire, Emily found herself caught between laughter and tears. The easy banter, the warmth of their friendship—it was a balm to her wounded heart.

"Now," Charlotte said, her voice soft yet earnest as she reached for Emily's hand, "tell us, truly, how have you been?"

Emily hesitated, her throat tightening. She glanced at Mathew, now engrossed in a book at the far end of the parlor, then back to her friends' concerned faces.

"I am... managing," she said, willing her voice not to waver.

"This is your third Christmas since becoming a widow. I can only imagine how it weighs on you." Beatrice leaned forward, her sharp features softening. "We are here for you, Em. Whatever you need."

"It has gotten easier with time." Emily offered a small grin.

Emily's gaze drifted to the window, where snowflakes danced in the fading light. She sighed, a wistful sound that did not escape her friends' notice.

"You seem... distant," Charlotte ventured, her

gaze filled with concern. "What is occupying your mind?"

Beatrice, ever observant, narrowed her eyes. "Or perhaps... who?"

Emily's cheeks flushed, and she fumbled with her teacup. "I-I do not know what you mean," she stammered, painfully aware of how unconvincing she sounded.

"Come now," Beatrice pressed, her tone softening despite her direct approach. "We have known you far too long to be fooled. There is a particular sorrow in your eye, one I have not seen since..."

"Since your husband was laid to rest," Charlotte finished, reaching out to squeeze Emily's hand.

Her heart clenched at the mention, though it was not her late husband that was causing her grief. She had tried so hard to push Nicolas from her thoughts, but now, faced with her friends' loving scrutiny, she felt her carefully constructed walls beginning to crumble.

"I met someone," Emily said, her fingers nervously tracing the delicate china. "He became injured during the blizzard, and I cared for him. Now..." Her voice faltered. "I can not stop thinking about him."

Charlotte sat her teacup down. "Does this someone have a name?"

Emily swallowed hard before saying, "Mr. Nicolas Winters."

"The notorious rogue with the playful smirks and dangerous smoldering gazes. No wonder you are in such a state," Beatrice said, fanning herself playfully.

Emily blew out a breath and sank back against the velvet upholstery. "It is foolish, I know. He left without a word, and yet..."

"And yet your heart still yearns," Charlotte supplied, her empathy evident in every word.

Beatrice leaned forward. "You deserve happiness, Emily," she said, her voice soft yet still resolute. "Perhaps it is time to consider opening your heart again."

"But what if—" Emily began, fear coloring her words.

"What if it leads to joy?" Charlotte interjected. "What if this is your second chance?"

Emily's gaze darted between her friends, their faces etched with care and encouragement. The tiny spark of hope she had tried to put out flickered anew, fragile but undeniably present.

"You are both too good to me," she said, a tremulous smile touching her lips.

Beatrice raised an eyebrow, a hint of her usual mischief returning. "Nonsense. We are simply reminding you of your own worth. Now, shall we plot your grand romantic gesture, or would you prefer another scone first?"

Emily laughed at Beatrice's quip, her spirits lifting ever so slightly. She reached for a scone, her fingers trembling as she broke off a piece. "I suppose... Well, maybe... I could write to him," she said.

Charlotte's gaze lit up. "That is a wonderful idea. A letter would allow you to express your feelings without the pressure of an immediate response."

"But what would I even say?" Emily's voice cracked with uncertainty, her brow furrowing. "How do I put into words... all that is in my heart?"

Beatrice leaned forward, her gaze intense. "Speak from your heart, darling. Tell him how he makes you feel, how your world is brighter when he is in it."

Emily nodded, her resolve strengthening. She rose from her seat and moved to her writing desk, pulling out a fresh sheet of paper. Her friends watched in supportive silence as she dipped her quill in ink and wrote.

"Dear Mr. Winters," she murmured as she penned the words, her heart racing. "I find myself compelled to write to you, for my thoughts have been consumed by our time together... I must speak with you once you have seen to your sister."

As Emily wrote, she felt a weight lifting from her

shoulders. She thought of stolen glances and shared laughter, of the warmth that bloomed within her whenever he was near. With each word, her determination grew.

I know not why you left as you did, she wrote, her quill scratching softly against the paper, but I cannot let fear or misunderstanding keep us apart. If there is even the slightest chance that you feel as I do, I implore you to respond. For I have found in you a renewed chance for happiness, and I am not ready to let that go.

Emily paused, her quill hovering over the paper. She glanced back at Charlotte and Beatrice, who offered encouraging smiles. Taking a deep breath, she turned back to her letter.

With hope and affection, she concluded, signing her name with a flourish.

As she folded the letter, Emily felt a curious mixture of trepidation and excitement. She had taken the first step toward her future, whatever it might hold.

With trembling fingers, she pressed her seal into the warm wax, watching as it hardened into a perfect crimson circle. She held the letter for a moment, its weight in her hands far greater than mere paper and ink.

"It is done," she breathed, turning to face Charlotte and Beatrice.

Charlotte clasped her hands together, eyes sparkling. "Oh, Emily, I am so proud of you. This is a monumental step."

Beatrice leaned forward, her lips curved with mischief. "Now, shall we summon your footman to deliver it, or shall I volunteer to play messenger? I daresay I could add a few choice words of my own to Mr. Winters."

Emily laughed, the sound surprising her with its lightness. "I am afraid I do not know where to send it. I know Mr. Winters was intent on reaching London, but do not know where in London he went. Though I appreciate the offer, Beatrice, I think it will take more than a standard messenger to ensure the letter reaches him."

Charlotte moved to her side, placing a comforting hand on her arm. "Perhaps send it on to the earl's residence? Mr. Winters is sure to at least stop in to see his parents for Christmas."

Emily paused, considering. "True," she admitted. "But... For the first time in so long, I feel as though I am moving forward rather than simply existing. I want this letter to reach him without delay."

Beatrice joined them, her usual sharp wit softened by genuine affection. "That is because you are, my dear. You are reclaiming your life, one daring letter at a time." She turned, her brow furrowed. "Now then, how are we to get this delivered without delay?"

"I shall write another letter. This time to the Wicked Widows Club. If anyone in London can locate Mr. Winters' post hate, it is the widows." Emily moved back to her desk, taking the quill in hand. "They are most helpful in times like this."

Once finished, she folded the new letter around the old one, sealed it, then rang for her footman to deliver the missives.

Once Emily dispatched Thomas with the missives, the three women gathered by the window, watching as he disappeared down the snow-dusted lane.

"Well," Emily said, turning back to her friends with a tremulous smile. "I suppose there is nothing left to do now... except wait."

"And celebrate," Beatrice declared, moving to the sideboard where a decanter of sherry waited. "This calls for a toast, I think."

As Beatrice poured three glasses, Charlotte squeezed Emily's hand. "Whatever comes of this, Emily, know that we are here for you. Always."

Emily felt a rush of gratitude. "I do not know what I would do without you both," she said softly.

Beatrice returned, glasses in hand. "Fortunately, you will never have to find out. Now, to new beginnings and brave hearts."

Optimism surged through Emily as they clinked their glasses together. The future was uncertain, but with friends like these by her side, she felt ready to face whatever it might bring.

As the golden light of the setting sun streamed through the frost-etched windows, Emily found herself lost in thought, her gaze fixed on the gentle flurries of snow outside. The warmth of the sherry lingered on her lips, a pleasant contrast to the chill that seemed to permeate the air despite the roaring fire in the hearth.

"I wonder," she mused aloud, her voice barely above a whisper, "how long it might take for the Wicked Widows to find him."

Charlotte, ever observant, placed a comforting hand on Emily's arm. "Patience, my dear. The wheels of fate turn at their own pace."

Beatrice, not one to let a moment of melancholy linger, clapped her hands together. "Speaking of wheels turning, shall we hang the last of the garlands? This room could use a touch more festivity, I think."

As they adorned the room with fragrant pine boughs and shimmering ribbons, Emily found her spirits lifting. The scent of cinnamon and cloves wafted from the kitchen, where cook was preparing their evening meal. While the warm glow of candle-light danced off the polished silver ornaments, casting playful shadows across the walls.

"There," Emily said, stepping back to admire their handiwork. "It is beginning to feel like a proper Christmas now."

Charlotte nodded. "Indeed. One can almost hear the sleigh bells in the distance."

As if on cue, the distant jingle of bells floated through the air, causing all three women to exchange startled glances.

"Surely not..." Emily breathed, her heart quick-ening as she moved toward the window.

Her breath fogged the cold windowpane as she peered out into the gathering dusk. The snow-dusted lane stretched empty before her. No sign of an approaching sleigh or carriage.

"False alarm, I am afraid," she said, turning back to her friends with a rueful smile. "Just my imagina-tion getting the better of me."

Beatrice arched a playful eyebrow. "Or perhaps it is your heart playing tricks on you. I have been told it has a tendency to do that when one is lovesick."

Emily's cheeks burned. "Bea. I am not—"

"Oh, come now," Charlotte interjected, her soft

voice filled with understanding. "There is no shame in it. We are your friends, Emily. We only want to see you happy."

Emily sank into a nearby armchair, the velvet upholstery cool against her flushed skin. "Is it that obvious?" she asked, her voice low. "Do you think Mathew noticed?"

Beatrice snorted, settling herself on the ottoman at Emily's feet. "My dear, you are about as subtle as a thunderstorm. Though I daresay Mathew has been too busy with his own pursuits to notice anything amiss."

"Bea," Charlotte chided, though her eyes danced with amusement. She perched on the arm of Emily's chair, wrapping a comforting arm around her friend's shoulders. "What she means to say is that there is nothing at all wrong with you. Love is a marvelous thing, and all of this will surely work out. Mr. Winters must love you as well, given what you have told us. It was probably fear that prevented him from saying farewell."

Emily's mind flashed back to that fateful evening before Nicolas left—the warmth of his embrace, the tenderness in his passionate gaze, the feeling that perhaps, just perhaps, she had found a second chance at love. Then came the crushing blow of waking to find him gone, nothing save for a brief note to prove he had been there at all.

"It does not signify," Emily said, forcing a lightness into her tone that she did not feel. "I have done all I can. There is nothing for it now, other than to wait."

Beatrice leaned forward, a glass of sherry in her hand. "Love is not always straightforward, Emily. Sometimes it requires time to work it's self out."

"Time." Emily sighed. "I do indeed have an abundance of that." Though she could not help but wonder how much of it she would spend waiting to hear from Nicolas. Waiting to see him. Waiting to discover if he cared at all.

She took a slow sip of sherry, her mind reliving the night she had spent in Nicolas's arms for the hundredth time. If she did not cease this, she would ruin Christmas with her woolgathering and melancholy.

But she could scarcely help how she felt.

All she wanted for Christmas was her rogue.

Charlotte took the empty glass from Emily's hand, a knowing glint in her eyes. "Christmas is known for miracles," she said, as she turned toward the sideboard.

Eleven

⤜⟡⤛

The wind howled fiercely as Nicolas pushed through the heavy oak door of the Thorne and Petal Inn, a swirl of snowflakes chasing after him. He stomped his boots, dislodging clumps of snow onto the worn floorboards, and shook his greatcoat with a vigor that sent droplets flying. His tousled dark hair, dampened by the softly falling snow, clung to his forehead in wayward curls.

"By Jove," he said, a spark of mischief flickering in his gaze despite the chill biting through his bones. He cast his gaze about the cozy common room, taking in the flickering candlelight and the inviting aroma of mulled wine. He had stopped here on his way to Blackwood's estate last month and found it quite welcoming.

The innkeeper, a portly man with ruddy cheeks, bustled over immediately. "Lord Winters. What a pleasant surprise to see you again. And so soon. Come, come, let us get you warmed up."

Nicolas grinned, unable to resist a bit of playful banter. "My good man, are you implying I have taken leave of my senses? Venturing out on a day like this does indeed suggest madness. Though I assure you, my reputation for mischief has not quite reached such heights."

The innkeeper chuckled, clearly accustomed to Nicolas' behavior. "Never would I suggest such a thing, my lord. Though I must say, your timing is impeccable. I have a prime spot by the fire, just perfect for thawing out a wayward gentleman."

As Nicolas followed the innkeeper to a comfortable armchair near the crackling hearth, His thoughts inevitably drifted to Emily. Was she thinking of him, too? Each mile brought him closer, yet still, the distance between them lingered in his heart. The warmth of the fire seeped into his chilled limbs, but it could not compare to the warmth he felt when he pictured her smile.

"Now then, my lord," the innkeeper said, interrupting his musings, "what can I get you to chase away the cold? Perhaps a hot meal to go with that seat by the fire? And will you be needing a room?"

Nicolas settled into the chair, stretching his long legs toward the flames. "Food sounds marvelous. I daresay I have worked up quite an appetite on my journey." His stomach growled in agreement, and he could not help but chuckle at his body's impeccable timing. "But a room will not be necessary."

As the innkeeper hurried off to fetch a menu, Nicolas gazed into the dancing flames, his mind once again turning to Emily. He had traversed snow-dusted roads and braved the biting wind, all for the chance to see her again. Would she welcome him with open arms, or would he be met with scorn? He could scarcely blame her if she was vexed at him. Still, he hoped for a welcome embrace. The uncertainty gnawed at him, but he pushed it aside. After all, he was no stranger to risk.

"Soon, my darling," he whispered, a determined smile playing at the corners of his mouth. "Soon, we shall meet again, and perhaps this time, I will get it right."

He inhaled deeply, savoring the tantalizing aroma of roasted meat and freshly baked bread that wafted through the inn. His stomach rumbled again, more insistently this time.

"I will have your heartiest stew, good sir," he called out to the innkeeper, his voice carrying a hint of his customary charm. "And a generous helping of that heavenly-smelling bread, if you please."

The innkeeper nodded with approval. "Excellent choice, my lord. Our lamb stew is renowned in these parts. It will warm you right up."

As he waited for his meal, Nicolas found his gaze drawn to a nearby table. A young woman sat there, her attention fixed upon him with unmistakable interest. She leaned over, offering him a view of her barely contained breasts as she gave a coy smile.

"Good evening, sir," she purred, her voice laden with invitation. "Are you traveling alone on this cold winter's day?"

Nicolas could not help but be amused by her forwardness. In another time, an invitation from such a woman would have stirred his interest, perhaps even been welcomed. But now... now there was Emily. And with that thought, the ache of longing bloomed anew. What was once tempting now paled compared to the woman who had captured his heart.

"I am afraid I am, madam," he replied, his tone friendly but reserved. "Though I hope not to be alone for much longer. I am on my way to visit... someone quite special."

A wistful smile played at the corners of his

mouth as he thought of Emily. "You see," he continued, his voice gentle but firm, "my heart belongs to another."

The woman's flirtatious smile faltered for a moment before she regained her composure. "How fortunate she must be." A hint of disappointment threaded through her voice.

Nicolas nodded, his thoughts already miles away. "It is I who am fortunate, madam. Now, if you will excuse me, I must finish my meal and continue my journey. I have a long way yet to go if I am to reach my lady in time for Christmas."

As he turned back to his food, he could not help but feel a surge of anticipation. Every bite, every moment, brought him closer to Emily. And with any luck at all, closer to a future he scarcely deserved, but most desperately craved.

❧

Back at the Fairfield estate, the parlor was alive with activity. Emily stood on tiptoe, reaching to hang a delicate glass ornament on a high branch of the towering Christmas tree.

"Mother, look," Mathew said, holding up a shimmering star. "Can I put this one at the very top?"

Emily's heart swelled with affection as she gazed

at Mathew. "Of course, just as soon as a footman brings the ladder."

Charlotte approached, her arms laden with garlands. "Where shall we drape these?"

"Perhaps along the mantelpiece?" Emily glanced around the room. "Beatrice, what do you think?"

Beatrice, halfway through arranging the candles, grinned, mischief lighting her eyes. "I think it a travesty that we have not drank the mulled wine yet. Decorating is thirsty work, after all."

Emily laughed, the sound tinged with both joy and a hint of melancholy. "You are incorrigible, Bea. But I suppose a little wine would not go amiss."

As Charlotte busied herself with the garlands and Beatrice went in search of refreshments, Emily gazed out the frost-covered window. The snow-laden landscape stretched out before her, and she could not help but wonder where Nicolas might be at that very moment.

Had her letter reached the Wicked Widows? If anyone could locate Nicolas, it was the widows, for they moved in scandalous circles. That letter might now be in his hands. Was it foolish to hope he might care enough to return? Could he even now be on his way to her? Or had he laughed as he tossed her words into the closest hearth and watched them incinerate?

"Mama?" Mathew's voice broke through her reverie. "Are you thinking about Papa again?"

Emily turned to her son, a bit unsettled by his perceptiveness, even if he had the wrong man. Emily went to him, smoothing his unruly hair. "Are you missing your father?"

"Not as much as I once did." An impish smile played at his mouth. "Does that make me a bad son?"

"Not at all, darling boy." She hugged him close. "It is hard not to think about those we have lost this time of year, but it has gotten easier for me as well. I think of your father and the time we spent together with fondness rather than sorrow these days."

"I mostly wonder if he would approve of me. Of who I am becoming." Mathew looked up at her. "Do I make as good a viscount as father did?"

Emily gave a genuine smile. "Your father would be proud as punch at the young man you are becoming. As for what kind of viscount you make... well, for a lad of twelve, you are doing an excellent job."

She took the ornament from him and turned toward the tree.

"Mother," he said.

She turned back to him.

"Will you marry again?"

Emily hesitated, biting her lip as uncertainty tugged at her heart. How could she explain the ache she felt without knowing if Nicolas would ever return her affections? Perhaps she should tell Mathew about Nicolas. But then what if it all came to nothing?

As if on cue, Beatrice burst back into the room, a tray of steaming mulled wine in her hands. "Ladies and young sir, I propose a contest. Whoever hangs the most ornaments in the next quarter-hour wins the honor of hanging the mistletoe above the door."

Charlotte gave a joyful grin. "What fun. Though I warn you, I have quite the eye for symmetry."

Laughter filled the room as they all reached for ornaments, their joy infectious. Emily found herself caught up in the merriment, her worries temporarily forgotten as she competed with her friends and son.

"No fair." Mathew laughed, stretching on his tiptoes to reach a higher branch. "Aunt Charlotte's arms are longer than mine."

"That will not be the case for long," Beatrice teased.

Emily watched the scene unfold, her heart swelling with both happiness and an undercurrent of sorrow. The twinkling candlelight reflected in her son's eyes, reminding her of the teasing glint that often danced in Nicolas's.

Her fingers traced the smooth curve of a silver bell, her thoughts drifting, imagining how Nicolas's laughter might fill the room, how his presence might chase away the lingering chill in her heart. She wondered if he had ever seen a Christmas tree and what he would make of it.

Emily took a deep breath, steeling herself against the melancholy threatening to overwhelm her. She forced a bright smile, determined to push aside her longing for Nicolas and focus on the present moment.

Their decorating competition soon transitioned into singing carols and as the last notes of "God Rest Ye Merry, Gentlemen" faded away, leaving a momentary hush in the parlor, Emily allowed her mind to wonder elsewhere.

"Your playing is simply divine," Charlotte said, admiration written across her features. "Shall we try 'The First Noel' next?"

Emily nodded, forcing her attention back to the present. "Of course. Mathew, would you be so kind as to turn the pages for me?"

As her son took his place beside her, Emily began the gentle introduction. Her gaze, however, could not help but drift toward the parlor window. She chided herself for such foolishness, yet her traitorous heart refused to obey.

"Mother." Mathew tapped her on the elbow. "You missed the start."

"My apologies," Emily said, finding her place. As she played, she let her thoughts wander. Tomorrow was Christmas Day, she mused. And here she was, acting like a lovesick girl, longing for the rogue who had left her. She had to stop this nonsense at once.

The group's voices rose in harmony, filling the room with a joyous sound. Beatrice's clear soprano soared above the rest, while Charlotte's rich alto provided a sturdy foundation. Even Mathew, his voice not yet changed, sang with infectious enthusiasm.

Emily joined in, her own voice steady despite her inner turmoil. "Noel, Noel, Noel, Noel, Born is the King of Israel..."

As the last verse approached, Emily found herself woolgathering again. Oh, Nicolas. Where are you this Christmas Eve? Do you think of me as I think of you?

She shook her head, trying to dispel such fanciful notions. Yet as the carol ended, she could not help but cast one more hopeful glance at the drive, her heart yearning for a Christmas miracle.

Emily's fingers lingered on the piano keys, her eyes closed as she savored the moment. The soft crackling of the fire and the gentle ticking of the mantel clock punctuated the silence.

The parlor door swung open and Emily startled

at the sound, turning toward it. There, framed by the warm glow of the firelight, a familiar figure stepped into the room—Nicolas, bringing with him the scent of bay rum and pine.

Emily's heart slammed against her ribs, her breath catching as her fingers froze above the piano keys. Surely she was imagining this. "Nicolas," she said, her voice a mere whisper.

Mathew wrapped his hand around her arm. "Mother, who is he?"

"He is a friend…" Emily's voice trailed off as the room erupted into a flurry of surprised exclamations and greetings, but Emily remained frozen in place, her gaze locked with Nicolas's. He moved toward her, a soft smile playing on his lips.

"My dear Lady Fairchild," he said, his tone playful yet tinged with an undercurrent of genuine emotion.

Emily's cheeks flushed, her heart pounding a wild rhythm.

"Mr. Winters," she said, her voice steadier than she felt. "What a... surprise."

There was no way her letter could have reached him before yesterday and he would not have been able to travel from London so fast. It could only mean one thing. He must have come of his own accord. But why?

Nicolas's smile widened. "I do so love to keep everyone on their toes."

As their eyes locked, Emily teetered on the edge of hope and uncertainty, torn between the joy of his unexpected return and the fear of what it might mean. Would Nicolas's presence bring the happiness she longed for, or would it lead to more heartache?

Twelve

❧

The heavy oak door of the parlor closed with a resounding thud, the sound echoing through the room like the toll of a bell, sealing them in. Beatrice and Charlotte's soft reassurances to Mathew faded into the hallway, leaving only the thick silence between Emily and Nicolas.

Emily stood frozen by the window, fingers clenched at her sides, as if tethering herself to the ground. Every fiber of her being screamed for her to close the distance between them, to feel his arms around her once more. Yet, fear held her back, an invisible wall she was not ready to breach. The very air seemed to crackle with tension, the only sound the fall of his boots against the plush Aubusson carpet as he approached.

"Emily..." Her name fell from his lips, the deep resonance of his voice wrapping around her, pulling her into its warmth even as she resisted. Her heart stuttered in response, betraying the fragile hold she had on her emotions. She willed herself to remain still, unwilling to face him, to see the regret etched upon that achingly handsome face.

She both longed for and feared his apology because she could not be certain what he was sorry for. Her heart would break anew if he shared regret over the time they spent together. But if he had come to declare his love... If he wished to express regret over the callous way he had left her... She pressed her eyelids closed and fought to maintain composure.

He halted a mere foot away, close enough that she could feel the heat radiating off his body, smell the hint of bay rum that always clung to his skin. "Emily, please. Look at me."

She blew out a measured breath, then turned, slowly, deliberately, lifting her chin in silent defiance even as her treacherous heart hammered against her ribs. His eyes blazed with intensity, the lines of his face drawn in contrition.

"I owe you more than an apology," he began, his voice thick with emotion. "What I did... leaving you that way... it was unforgivable. I let my fear control me, and in doing so, I hurt the one person I can not live without."

Her breath hitched, anger and hurt swirling within her. She wanted to cling to her righteous indignation, but his words chipped away at her defenses, leaving her exposed, raw. Emily searched his face, torn between the pain he had caused and the overwhelming love she felt.

She had spent countless nights replaying their last hours together, dissecting every word, every gesture, searching for some glimmer of the affection she had once been so sure he held for her. And now he was here. Standing before her. Declaring his feelings.

Nicolas took a tentative step closer, his hand lifting as if to touch her cheek before falling back to his side. "I was a fool, Emily. A coward. I did what I have always done without realizing how deep my affection for you ran. I disappeared without a farewell, convinced that I was unworthy of you, that I would only bring you pain. But in my haste to protect you, I realize now that I inflicted a far greater wound."

Tears pricked at the corners of her eyes, her vision blurring as a maelstrom of emotions swirled within her breast. The hurt, the anger, the love and longing—all warred for dominance, threatening to overwhelm her.

"Can you ever forgive me?" he whispered, his voice raw with vulnerability. "I know I have no right to ask for your absolution, but I swear to you, on all that I hold dear, that I will spend the rest of my days proving myself worthy of your trust, your affection...your love."

Emily's heart constricted painfully, the sincerity in his words, the naked emotion in his gaze chipping away at the walls she had erected around her battered heart.

As if sensing her internal struggle, Nicolas closed the remaining distance between them, his hands gently grasping her trembling fingers. The warmth of his touch sent a shiver down her spine, and she instinctively leaned into his proximity, drawn by the magnetism that had always existed between them.

"Emily," he breathed, his voice a reverent caress. "You have changed me in ways I never thought possible. Your strength, your compassion, your unwavering grace—they have shown me what true love really means. You have become the very center of my world, the beating heart that gives my life purpose and meaning. I am lost to you. Completely and irrevocably in love with you."

His words washed over her like a soothing balm, easing the ache that had taken root in her soul. In the depths of his gaze, she saw a reflection of her own longing, a yearning for a love that transcended all boundaries.

"I love you, Emily Fairchild." His voice was soft yet filled with the weight of a million unspoken promises. "I love you with every part of me—more than I thought myself capable of. You are my light, my heart... and I was too blind to see it before... I love you with every fiber of my being, with a passion that burns brighter than the stars themselves. I know I have made mistakes, that I have caused you pain. But I swear to you, I will spend the rest of my life making it right. If you will have me, I promise to cherish you, to support you, to be the man you deserve by your side."

Emily's throat constricted, her heart racing as the weight of his declaration settled upon her. She searched his face, seeking the truth behind his words, and found only pure, unadulterated love shining back at her. It was a love that promised healing, that offered a chance at a future she had once thought lost forever.

She closed her eyes, drawing in a shaky breath as she wrestled with the decision that lay before her. To forgive, to give her heart once more, was to risk the very fabric of her being. But to turn away, to deny the love that burned so fiercely between them, would be to condemn herself to a lifetime of regret and longing.

"Emily," he said, his voice hoarse with emotion. "I know I have no right to ask, but I am still a selfish man. I want you for myself. Today, tomorrow, always. I am asking you to marry me, Emily. I want to spend the rest of my life proving that you made the right choice in loving me. Let me be your partner, your protector, your husband. Let me be the man you deserve."

Her eyes fluttered open. In the depths of her gaze, he saw a glimmer of the future he so desperately longed for, a future filled with love, laughter, and the promise of forever.

She took a step forward, her hand trembling as she reached out to caress his cheek. The warmth of his skin beneath her fingertips sent a shiver down her spine, igniting a fire within her.

"Nicolas..." Her voice trembled, betraying the storm raging inside her. "I am terrified to trust again, to believe that this—" she gestured between them, her hand trembling "—can be real. What if we fall apart? What if you leave me again?" She averted her gaze for a heartbeat, then continued. "Still, I cannot deny the truth that resides within my heart. I love you with a depth and intensity that frightens me. I have longed for this since the very moment I reached for you, only to find you gone." She drew in a breath. "My heart shattered at the loss. Still, I do not want to live a life where I wonder what if. I would rather face that fear with you."

He leaned into her touch, reveling in the softness of her hand. "Let me be your strength, your solace. Together, we can face any obstacle, overcome any fear. I vow I will never leave you again. Never willingly cause you a moment's pain."

The walls she had constructed around her heart crumbled in the face of his unwavering devotion. In that moment, she knew that the risk was one worth taking, that the promise of a future with Nicolas outweighed the fears that held her captive.

"Yes." Tears slipped down her cheeks as she gazed at him. "Yes, Nicolas. I will marry you."

He gathered her in his arms, his lips finding hers in a kiss that sealed their fate, a promise of a love that would endure through the ages. And as they clung to each other, their hearts beating as one, he knew they had found their home, their haven, in the shelter of each other's embrace.

The door burst open, and in rushed Beatrice, Charlotte, and Mathew, their faces a mix of surprise and delight. Beatrice was the first to recover, her eyes glinting with amusement. "Well, I see we are just in time for the happy ending," she quipped, her sharp gaze softening as it landed on Emily and Nicolas.

Charlotte, her blonde curls bouncing with each step, clasped her hands together in delight. "Oh, Emily," she said, her voice filled with genuine happiness. "I am so thrilled for you both."

Mathew, his chestnut-brown hair tousled from the excitement, grinned from ear to ear. "Mother, Mr. Winters." He nodded, his expression filled with a mix of youthful exuberance and sincere affection. "Aunt Beatrice and Aunt Charlotte filled me in. I suppose congratulations are now in order."

Emily and Nicolas, still wrapped in each other's embrace, turned to face their impromptu audience. Emily's cheeks flushed with a becoming pink, her hazel eyes sparkling with a mixture of embarrassment and joy. "I suppose there is no hiding it now," she said, her voice trembling as she fought to contain her emotions.

Nicolas, his arm still securely around her waist, chuckled. "It seems our secret is out," he said, his gaze brimming with mirth. "And I am not the least bit ashamed."

Beatrice stepped forward and enveloped Emily in a fierce hug. "I knew you would bring him up to scratch," she said, her voice laced with affection. "I am so happy for you, Emily." Her sharp gaze softened for just a moment as she took in her friend's radiant expression. "You deserve this, Emily."

Charlotte approached Nicolas with a warm smile. "Congratulations, Mr. Winters," she said, her gaze filled with sincerity. "I trust you will make Emily incredibly happy."

Mathew stepped forward, a mixture of pride and vulnerability in his eyes. He squared his shoulders, his voice steady despite his youth. "Mr. Winters," he began, his voice carrying a blend of the politeness instilled by his upbringing and the informal cadence of an adolescent eager to assert his position. "I believe a formal introduction is in order. I am Mathew Fairchild, Viscount Gilford."

Nicolas, understanding the importance of this moment, disentangled himself from Emily's embrace and turned to face the young lord. He bowed, a gesture of respect and deference, before meeting Mathew's gaze with a sincere expression. "It is an honor to make your acquaintance, Lord Gilford. I have heard so much about you from your mother, and I must say, her pride in you is well-founded."

Mathew's cheeks flushed at the compliment, but he maintained his composure, determined to fulfill his role as the protector of his family. "I appreciate your kind words, Mr. Winters." His voice remained steady despite the weight of the moment. "However, I must ask about your commitment to my mother. She has been through a great deal, and her happiness is of the utmost importance to me."

Nicolas nodded, his gaze filled with understanding. He took a step closer to Mathew, his posture open and honest. "Lord Gilford, I assure you that my intentions toward your mother are nothing short of honorable," he began, his voice filled with conviction. "I have come to realize that Emily is the most extraordinary woman I have ever known, and I am deeply in love with her. I want nothing more than to spend the rest of my life making her happy and cherishing her as she deserves."

Mathew listened intently, his gaze never wavering from Nicolas' face. "Mr. Winters," Mathew said, his voice softening, "I give you my blessing."

Nicolas lowered himself to one knee, leveling his gaze with Mathew's. "Lord Gilford, I give you my word. I will protect and love your mother with everything I have."

With a slow nod, Mathew's face softened into a smile. "I believe you," he began, his voice slightly tremulous, "And I welcome you into our family."

Nicolas reached out to clasp Mathew's hand, a gesture of gratitude and understanding passing between them. "Thank you, Lord Gilford," he said, his voice thick with emotion. "I promise to be not only a devoted husband to your mother, but also a loyal and supportive friend to you."

Nicolas wrapped an arm around Mathew's shoulders, pulling him into a warm, fatherly embrace. Emily's heart swelled with love as she watched them, knowing that this was the family she had always longed for.

As Nicolas and Mathew shared a moment of silent camaraderie, Beatrice and Charlotte exchanged knowing glances, their eyes sparkling with delight at the touching scene unfolding before them. With a gentle clearing of her throat, Beatrice stepped forward, mischief dancing across her features. "Well, now that the formalities are out of the way," she said, her voice laced with a playful lilt, "perhaps we should give the lovebirds some privacy?"

Charlotte, her soft features alight with under-standing, nodded in agreement. "Indeed, Bea," she said, her voice warm and gentle. "I believe Emily and Mr. Winters have much to discuss." Turning to Mathew, she said, "Shall we adjourn to our chambers? The hour grows late and morning will bring Christmas Day."

Mathew offered an agreeable nod. "An excellent

suggestion," he agreed, his youthful face alight with a mix of happiness and a touch of reluctance to leave his mother's side. With a final glance at her, he allowed Beatrice and Charlotte to guide him from the room.

Thirteen

As the parlor stilled, silence wrapped around them. Alone at last, the world beyond their shared moment seemed to fade into insignificance. Emily's heart thrummed, her eyes shimmering with unshed tears of joy as she gazed up at Nicolas. How improbable it all seemed—that this man, the one she had longed for, now stood before her, love etched so clearly on his face.

Her Christmas wish had come true, and as fate would have it, she did not need to do anything at all, for he came of his own accord. Nicolas truly loved her.

His hand rose with a tenderness that stole her breath, his fingers trailing over her cheek. "My darling Emily," he whispered, his voice thick with emotion, "when shall we begin forever? When would you like to become my wife?"

Emily, her heart fluttering, leaned into his touch, savoring the warmth and strength of his presence. "As soon as the banns can be read," she said, her voice trembling with emotion, "I have dreamed of this moment, and now that it is here, I have no desire to delay."

He pulled her against him. "Thank goodness, for I have no wish to wait, either. I would marry this very night if I could."

Nicolas's gaze flicked upward, a playful smile tugging at his lips as he nodded toward the sprig of mistletoe hanging above them. "It seems even the heavens conspire to keep us together, my love."

Emily, her cheeks flushed with anticipation, tipped her head back, her gaze locked with his. As he leaned in, his lips mere inches from hers, she could feel the warmth of his breath mingling with her own, sending shivers of delight down her spine.

When their lips met, it was as though every unsaid word, every moment of longing, poured into the kiss. The only sound was their ragged breathing and the pounding of their hearts as they clung to each other, the depth of their love wrapped in that singular moment.

She threaded her fingers through his hair as she lost herself in the magic of the moment.

As they parted, their breathing ragged and their hearts racing, he rested his forehead against hers. "I love you, my dearest Emily, and I will love you until the end of my days... beyond, if the fates allow."

She smiled up at him, her eyes sparkling. "And I love you, Nicolas Winters," she asked, her voice soft and filled with wonder. "I never dreamed I could find such happiness again, but you have shown me that love can indeed conquer all."

"Indeed it can." Nicolas hugged her closer. "How would you like to spend the first night of the rest of our lives?" He asked, a playful grin curving his full lips.

"Hum…" Emily mussed, glancing toward the stairway visible just beyond the parlor door. "I have a few ideas."

Her playful suggestion hung in the air, charged with anticipation. Nicolas's eyes darkened with desire, but he took a deep breath, steadying himself.

"My dearest," he said, brushing a stray curl from her cheek, "nothing would bring me greater joy than to whisk you upstairs this very moment. But you deserve better. At the least, you deserve to be properly wed, and I mean to do things right this time."

Her lips curved into a teasing smile. "How very

noble of you, Mr. Winters. And here I thought your reputation as a rake was well-earned."

He chuckled, pulling her close. "Ah, but you have reformed me, my love. I aim to be a gentleman worthy of your hand."

"And if I prefer the scoundrel I feel in love with?" Emily's voice was a sultry whisper, her fingers tracing the lapels of his coat with teasing intent.

His pulse quickened, his resolve nearly crumbling under the weight of her seduction. But he held fast, drawing a shaky breath. "You make me want to be a better man, Emily. To do right by you in every way."

"And you make me want to be a scandalous woman," she said, her tone laced with desire.

"Incorrigible minx." Nicolas swept her off her feet, cradling her in his muscular arms as he carried her toward the staircase. Her tinkling laughter filled the air, her heart racing with anticipation as she clung to his broad shoulders. The warmth of his body seeped through the layers of her gown, igniting a fire within her that burned with the intensity of a thousand suns.

As they ascended the stairs, Emily's mind raced with the scandalous possibilities that awaited them. Her cheeks flushed a becoming pink, and she buried her face in the crook of his neck, breathing in his intoxicating scent.

She had never felt so alive, so consumed by the desire and love that coursed through her. Feathering her fingers through the hair at his nape, she pressed a kiss to his neck.

Nicolas's resolve wavered as her teasing touch ignited a fire deep within him. He longed to possess her, to lose himself in her completely. But he could not—would not—allow himself to fall. Not yet. His love for her demanded patience, respect, and honor, even when every fiber of his being screamed otherwise.

At the landing, Nicolas hesitated, his gaze locking with hers before he turned toward her bedchamber. With a tender kick, he opened the door and carried her inside, lowering her onto the plush bedcovers as though she were something precious, fragile even. The reverence in his gaze stole her breath.

"My darling," he said, his voice low and filled with longing. "As much as I burn for you, my love." He caressed her cheek with longing. "I cannot take you to my bed again until we are bound in marriage. You deserve every honor, every promise of devotion that I can give. I will not betray that."

Her heart brimmed with admiration, her love for him deepening in ways she had not thought possible.

His restraint, his devotion, only made her ache for him more. But she knew that when the time came, it would be all the more perfect for the waiting.

She reached up to caress his cheek, her gaze shining with affection. "My dearest Nicolas," she said, "your honor and respect mean more to me than any fleeting passion. Though I confess, the temptation is great indeed."

He leaned into her touch, pressing a kiss to her palm.

"I swear to you, Emily," Nicolas said, his voice laced with desire, "when we are wed, I will worship every inch of you, body and soul. I will make you mine in every way imaginable, and you will know pleasures you have never dreamed of."

A delicious shiver ran through her at his words, and she offered a coy smile. "I shall hold you to that promise, my dear Mr. Winters."

He groaned, clearly battling his self-control. "You test me sorely, my love. But I will not yield." He leaned down, capturing her lips in a searing kiss that left her breathless and aching for more. But as quickly as it began, he pulled away, his eyes dark with restrained passion. "Goodnight, my sweet Emily," he said, his voice rough with emotion.

With one last lingering look, he turned and left the room, closing the door softly behind him. Emily sank back against the pillows, a blissful smile playing across her lips as she hummed a joyful tune. Her heart was so full of love and happiness that she thought it might burst from her chest.

As she drifted off to sleep, her thoughts were filled with visions of her future with Nicolas, of the life they would build together, and of the endless love they would share. For the first time in years, she knew she had found her true home, not in a place, but in the arms of the man who had captured her heart and made her believe in the power of second chances.

Tomorrow would bring the joy of Christmas morning, the warmth of family, and the promise of new beginnings. And soon after, there would be the reading of the banns, the vows exchanged, and the life she had scarcely dared to hope for. Her heart soared with the certainty that love had, indeed, conquered all.

Fourteen

E mily awoke with a contented smile, her heart fluttering as memories of the previous night filled her mind—Nicolas's tender words, his warm embrace, and the promise of their future together. Today felt like a promise in itself, a fresh start wrapped in the beauty of the season.

Christmas's past had held a bittersweet ache, a reminder of all she had lost. But this year... this year, it was a symbol of all she had found. Love, hope, and a future that sparkled like the snow outside her window.

Eager to join her family downstairs, she dressed with hurried excitement. As she descended the grand staircase, the familiar scents of cinnamon and pine wafted through the house, accompanied by the joyful sound of laughter echoing from the parlor. The air itself seemed to hum with the festive energy of Christmas morning.

She paused in the doorway, taking in the sight before her. Mathew sat cross-legged by the tree, his face alight with boyish excitement as he examined a brightly wrapped package. Beatrice and Charlotte huddled together on the settee, whispering and giggling like schoolgirls. And there, standing tall and handsome by the fireplace, was Nicolas.

His gaze found hers the moment she entered the doorway, his smile spreading like sunshine over her heart. "Merry Christmas, my love," he said, crossing the room in long, graceful strides, his presence filling the space between them. He took her hand, pressing a tender kiss to her knuckles.

Emily's cheeks flushed. "Merry Christmas, Nicolas."

"Mother," Mathew called, breaking the spell between them. "Come see what Father Christmas has brought."

Mathew's wide-eyed grin was contagious, his excitement infectious as he tugged her toward the tree. Seeing him so carefree, his laughter ringing out, warmed her very soul. It was as though the final piece of her world had clicked into place, with Nicolas now beside them.

Emily allowed herself to be pulled into the room, swept up in the joy and excitement of Christmas morning. As presents were exchanged and exclaimed over, she could not help but marvel at how different this Christmas was from the last. Gone was the loneliness and sorrow that had plagued her for so long. In its place was a warmth and contentment she had scarcely dared to hope for.

As the morning wore on, the group gathered around the fireplace, sipping chocolate and sharing stories. Nicolas's laughter filled the room, his eyes twinkling as he recounted his mischievous schoolboy antics. Mathew was enthralled, hanging on every word, and Emily delighted in the sight.

Nicolas had seamlessly slipped into this role—not as a replacement for Mathew's father, but as someone who could share in their lives, in their joy and laughter, as well as their sorrows.

"You should have seen the look on old Finch's face when he realized his wig was missing." Nicolas chuckled. "He searched the entire dormitory, never once thinking to look up at the chandelier where we had hung it."

Mathew howled with laughter, nearly spilling his chocolate. "Did you get caught?"

Nicolas winked. "Never."

Beatrice shook her head, a fond smile playing on

her lips. "I shudder to think what mischief you will inspire in our young Mathew. Though I daresay a bit of harmless fun never hurt anyone."

Charlotte laughed. "Indeed. I believe a touch of mischief is essential for a well-rounded education."

Emily shook her head, unable to suppress her own smile.

"Only the best kind, I assure you," Nicolas said with a merry grin as he squeezed Emily's hand in tender reassurance.

A sudden commotion at the door drew everyone's attention. The butler entered, looking somewhat flustered.

"My apologies for the interruption," he announced, "but Lord and Lady Quinton, his and her grace, the Duke and Duchess of Langley, and Viscount Brantford have arrived. They are accompanied by... a vicar, ma'am."

Emily's heart raced, her gaze meeting Nicolas's. The air in the parlor seemed to crackle with anticipation and bewilderment.

"Show them in," Emily said, rising to her feet.

As the unexpected guests entered, Emily's gaze fell upon the vicar standing amongst them, his hand holding what appeared to be a special license. Her breath caught, the air around her stilling. Could it be? Her eyes darted to Nicolas, finding the same blend of shock and excitement mirrored in his expression. The realization struck her like a wave, her heart leaping with joy.

Lord Quinton cleared his throat. "Well, my boy," he addressed Nicolas, "we could wait no longer to have Lady Fairchild join the family. What say you to a Christmas wedding?"

A collective gasp filled the room, followed by an eruption of excited chatter. Emily felt her cheeks flush as she looked at Nicolas, who was already striding toward her, his face alight with joy.

"My darling," he said, taking her hands in his, "shall we oblige them?"

Emily's heart soared. "Yes," she said, barely able to contain her happiness. "There is nothing I want more."

Charlotte let out a squeal of delight, clasping her hands together. "Oh, Emily. We must ready you at once."

Beatrice was already tugging at Emily's arm. "Come, come. We have not a moment to lose. You simply cannot be married in your day dress."

"I brought an orange blossom wreath for your hair," Lady Quinton said, stepping forward, Joslyn at her side.

As the ladies whisked Emily away, she glimpsed Nicolas's radiant smile. Her stomach flittered, a mixture of nerves and excitement surging through her.

Once in her chamber, Emily found herself at the center of a whirlwind of activity. Charlotte fussed with her hair, arranging pieces that had gone astray, while Beatrice rummaged through Emily's wardrobe.

"Ah, this will be perfect," Beatrice said, her eyes gleaming as she pulled out a gown of ivory silk with delicate red rosettes. "You will look like a vision, Emily—he will not be able to take his eyes off you."

As Emily changed, she could not help but marvel at the turn of events. "I can scarcely believe this is happening," she confessed, her voice trembling with emotion.

Charlotte paused in her ministrations, meeting Emily's gaze in the mirror. "My dear friend, you deserve all the happiness in the world. And Nicolas... well, he looks at you as if you are a priceless gem."

Emily felt tears prick at her eyes, overwhelmed by the love surrounding her. As Beatrice helped her into the gown, she caught sight of herself in the mirror. The ivory silk draped elegantly over her figure, the simplicity of the design lending her an air of timeless grace.

"We must not forget flowers," Joslyn, Duchess of Langley, said, dashing to the dressing table where her mother had laid the orange blossom wreath. She returned to Emily's side, then placed the wreath on her head, winding a few curls around it.

As the ladies stepped back, Emily took a deep breath, steadying herself. "I am ready," she announced, her voice filled with quiet determination and joy.

Her heart fluttered as she stepped into the parlor, her gaze seeking Nicolas. He stood before the vicar, his tall frame silhouetted against the flickering firelight. Mathew stood at his side looking every bit the lord of the house.

As her gaze met Nicolas's, she saw a flash of awe and tenderness in his deep green eyes that made her breath catch.

Nicolas's chest tightened as Emily approached, her beauty amplified by the soft glow of candles and the radiant smile that graced her lips. He extended his hand, unable to suppress a slight tremor as she placed her delicate fingers in his.

"Dearly beloved," the vicar began, his voice steady and warm.

Emily locked gazes with Nicolas. He stared back at her with an expression of earnest devotion that made her heart swell.

His hand trembled slightly as he took hers, his usual grin softening into something deeper, more heartfelt. "I, Nicolas," he began, his voice thick with emotion, "take thee, Emily, to be my wedded wife, my heart's truest companion, from now until forever…" His eyes never left hers, and for a moment, it was just the two of them, bound by words that held the promise of forever.

As Nicolas recited his vows, she felt tears of joy threatening to spill. She blinked them back, determined to commit every detail of this moment to memory.

"To have and to hold," he continued, his thumb tracing gentle circles on the back of her hand, "from this day forward, for better, for worse..."

Beatrice and Lady Quinton dabbed at their eyes with handkerchiefs, while Charlotte and Joslyn beamed with pride and joy. The men stood sentinel, their gazes shining with approval and warmth while Mathew rocked back on his heels, a barely contained smile threatening to break free.

Happy tears threatened to spill forth as Emily spoke her vows. "I, Emily, take thee, Nicolas, to be my wedded husband..." Her voice faltered, not from hesitation, but from the overwhelming joy that surged within her. At long last, the aching loneliness she had carried in her heart was replaced by something far more beautiful—a love that was steady, enduring, and true.

Nicolas's throat tightened as he listened to her words, marveling at how this remarkable woman had captured his heart so completely. He was filled with a profound sense of reverence for the moment and the woman before him.

As they exchanged rings, their fingers intertwined, both feeling the weight of the promises they had just made. The vicar's final proclamation was met with a swell of affection from those gathered, but for Emily and Nicolas, the world had narrowed to just the two of them, united at last.

The room erupted in joyous applause. Emily's heart lifted, soaring as Nicolas pulled her into his arms. His lips met hers in a kiss that was both tender and bold, a kiss that spoke of promises kept, of devotion unshaken.

"My darling wife," he said, tasting the words for the first time. "I do believe we have caused quite the stir this Christmas Day."

Emily's fingers tightened around his. "Indeed, we have, my dearest husband. And I could not imagine a more perfect Christmas."

As they turned to face their loved ones, the outpouring of affection overwhelmed Emily. She dabbed at a tear as slid down her cheek.

"Oh, Emily," Beatrice exclaimed, a bright smile

etched across her face. "You make such a beautiful bride."

Joslyn nodded in agreement. "And on Christmas Day, no less. How wonderfully romantic."

The celebration continued well into the evening, with toasts and laughter filling the air. As the clock struck midnight, Nicolas took Emily's hand, leading her away from the dwindling party.

In the quiet intimacy of their chamber, his lips grazed the tender skin of her shoulder. "My love," he said, his voice low and seductive, his fingers slowly unfastening the delicate buttons of her gown. "I intend to make this night magical beyond your wildest dreams."

Her breath caught as she felt the brush of his fingertips against her skin. "Nicolas," she whispered, "I never dared hope for such happiness."

"This is but the beginning, my dear. I have a lifetime of wicked delights planned for you."

Her fingers trembled as she reached for him, tracing the contours of his lean, athletic form.

Their lips met in a passionate kiss, tender yet filled with urgency. He guided her to their bed, laying her down with utmost care. His body covered hers, warm and solid, as he showered her with gentle kisses.

"I have dreamt of this moment," she confessed.

Nicolas smiled against her skin. "As have I, my love. And now I intend to make those dreams a reality. All. Night. Long."

His hands traced gentle patterns across her skin, his eyes dark with desire. "Tonight, my love," he said, his voice low and reverent, "we begin our forever." Her breath hitched as his lips found hers.

With adoring touches and whispered endearments, they explored each other, their bodies becoming one. Her body trembled with need as he pressed into her, calming her and igniting her soul. And when they reached their peak, he captured her lips in a devastating kiss as they tumbled over the edge together.

As they lay entwined, basking in the afterglow of their lovemaking, Emily felt a profound sense of contentment. She nestled closer to Nicolas, savoring the warmth of his embrace. "I believe we have found our happily ever after."

"Indeed, we have, my beloved wife." He pressed a soft kiss to her forehead. "And this, my darling, is just the first night of forever."

Epilogue

Fifteen years later...

Emily stood before her expansive mahogany wardrobe, her delicate hands folding gowns of various hues and textures. The soft rustle of silk and muslin filled the air as she placed each garment into the large wicker basket at her feet. As the years had passed, life had unfolded in a flurry of seasons, but each morning in their home still brought her a deep sense of peace. Today, however, there was a quiet nostalgia in the air—a reminder of how far she and Nicolas had come, of the life they had built together.

She paused, her fingers lingering on a lavender

day dress, the fabric smooth and cool under her touch. Alice will adore this, she thought as she folded the frock. Emily was certain their faithful maid would delight in the gown's simple elegance.

The floorboards outside her chamber creaked, and before she could turn, Emily felt the familiar presence of the man who had long since claimed her heart. The door swung open, and Nicolas stepped inside, the light from the hallway framing his tall figure. He filled the room with warmth even before his voice reached her ears.

"My love," he called, his tone carrying that familiar hint of mischief she adored. "Sorting through old gowns, are we?"

She turned to face him, her heart skipping as it always did at the sight of his roguish grin and tousled dark hair. "Nicolas," she said, her voice filled with delight. "I was not expecting you until this evening."

He leaned casually against the doorframe, his green eyes twinkling with affection. "Ah, my dear Emily, surely you know by now that I delight in the unexpected." He took a step closer, his gaze sweeping over her figure, his appreciation evident in the way his eyes lingered.

Emily felt a blush rise to her cheeks as she smoothed the front of her gown. "You have caught me in a rather undignified state." She gestured to the pile of gowns and the wicker basket at her feet.

Nicolas crossed the room in a few easy strides, his hands reaching out to tuck a loose curl behind her ear. "Nonsense," he said, his voice warm with affection. "You look as enchanting as ever." His fingers lingered against her cheek, and she leaned into his touch, the simple gesture filling her with a familiar excitement.

"You flatter me, sir," she said, though the flutter in her heart betrayed her calm exterior. "But I doubt you hurried home to watch me sort through old dresses."

Nicolas's grin widened. "Perhaps I did," he said, his voice dropping as he stepped closer. "Though I must admit, I am far more interested in what lies beneath those gowns." His hand brushed her waist, pulling her toward him.

Emily gasped, swatting him playfully on the arm. "Incorrigible as always." She laughed, but her smile softened as she gazed up at him, the years of love between them clear in every glance, every touch.

"And you love me for it," he said, pressing a kiss to her cheek, his voice low and tender.

"I do," she said, her heart swelling with affection. "More than you know."

They stood together in comfortable silence,

wrapped in the warmth of each other's presence. Emily's gaze drifted to the ivory silk gown folded beside her, the red rosettes along the bodice catching the sunlight. She ran her fingers over the delicate embroidery, her thoughts wandering back to the day she had worn it—the day that had changed her life forever.

"This gown…brings back such fond memories." Her voice trembled with the weight of emotion as the memories of their Christmas wedding flooded her mind. "It was the beginning of everything."

His eyes softened as he covered her hand with his. "You cannot give this away," he said, his voice quiet but firm. "It is more than just a dress, Emily. It is a symbol of the life we built, of the promises we made." His eyes met hers, a spark of emotion flickering in their depths. "Someday, our Mary will wear this gown, and we will tell her the story of how her parents stood before a Christmas fire and vowed to love each other for eternity."

Emily's breath caught at the tenderness in his words, her heart swelling with love. "Mary." She pictured their daughter's bright eyes and infectious laughter. "She would adore that."

Nicolas smiled, his gaze filled with affection. "Our daughter has a flair for drama, just like her mother. She will treasure this gown, as we have."

Her hand trembled as she set the gown aside. She turned toward Nicolas, her chest tightening with a swell of emotion. "You have given me so much, Nicolas," she said, her voice catching in her throat. "More than I ever thought possible. Our children, this home, the love we share... it is all I have ever dreamed of."

His fingers traced her cheek, his gaze tender and filled with adoration. "And you have given me more than I ever deserved, my love. You saved me from myself. You brought light into my life when all I knew was darkness." He leaned down, brushing his lips over hers. "I am forever grateful."

As their kiss deepened, Emily's heart raced, her body coming alive under his touch. The years had not dulled their passion, and every moment with Nicolas still felt as thrilling as their first. She melted into his embrace, her fingers threading through his hair as his hands traced the familiar curves of her body.

When they pulled apart, breathless and smiling, Nicolas's gaze darkened with desire. "Shall we make new memories, my love?" He brushed his lips against her neck.

Her laughter bubbled up, her hands tugging him closer. "Always the rogue," she teased, her voice filled with affection and anticipation. "Indeed, let us make more memories."

With a playful grin, he scooped her into his arms, carrying her toward the bed. "For you, my dearest Emily." He kissed her forehead. "I will always be the rogue who loves you beyond reason."

As they tumbled onto the bed, their laughter mingling with the soft rustle of sheets, Emily's heart soared. The years had been kind to them, and the love they shared had only grown deeper, more profound. This, she knew, was her forever—a life filled with love, laughter, and the promise of endless tomorrows with the man who had stolen her heart.

And as they lay entwined in each other's arms, Emily knew that no matter what the future held, they would face it together—side by side, as they always had. For theirs was a love that had weathered the storms of life and come out stronger, brighter, and more enduring than either of them had ever dreamed possible.

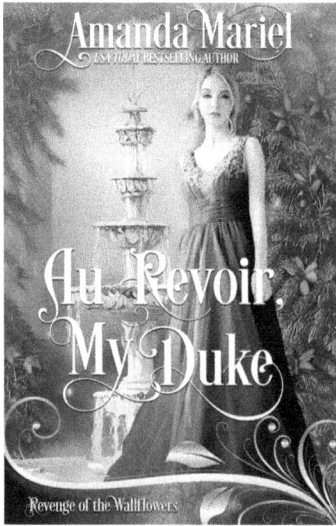

Keep reading for an excerpt from book 4 in the Regency Hearts Aflame series.

Lady Charlotte Ashbourne stands on the precipice of ruin, her family's fortune ruthlessly stolen by the enigmatic and brooding Duke of Ravenscroft, Grant Tilbury. Driven by desperation, Charlotte is determined to reclaim her family's honor and fortune from the man who ruined them.

Grant Tilbury, a notorious rogue, revels in a life of vice and leisure with no intentions of settling down. However, when he crosses paths with the spirited and beautiful Lady Charlotte, he finds himself intrigued. Unable to resist the challenge, he makes her an indecent proposal. Seeing an opportunity for revenge, Charlotte devises a daring plan: accept his indecent proposal, make him fall in love with her, bring him to his knees, and then shatter his heart as he did her family's.

As Christmas magic weaves its spell, the boundaries between pretense and reality begin to blur. Charlotte finds herself unexpectedly drawn to Grant, discovering hidden depths and vulnerabilities in him that she never anticipated. Grant, too, is captivated by Charlotte's fiery spirit and unyielding determination, finding himself entangled in emotions he thought he'd forever forsaken.

With secrets unveiled and their game of hearts taking an unexpected turn, the holiday festivities become a backdrop for a passionate battle of wills. Will Charlotte's quest for vengeance be overtaken by an undeniable love? Can the rogue Duke find redemption in the embrace of the woman who sought to destroy him? As their hearts intertwine and the true spirit of the season works its magic, the fate of their love hangs in the balance. Will Charlotte bid adieu to the Duke forever, or will love triumph in the most unexpected of ways?

Chapter 1

The stillness of winter settled heavily over Riverwood Manor, as if the snow itself had stolen away every sound. Even the crackling fire in the main hall seemed muted, the warmth barely touching the chill that seeped into Lady Charlotte Ashbourne's very bones.

She stood by the window, her bright eyes fixed on the snow-covered landscape. The flakes swirled and danced, beautiful yet cold—a reflection of the bleakness that had seeped into her bones. Her delicate features, once the epitome of grace and warmth, were now etched with a mix of anger and steely determination. A faint furrow in her brow hinted at the burden she carried.

"How far we have fallen," she murmured, her gloved fingers tracing the delicate pattern of frost on the windowpane. Once, Riverwood had been a place of glittering balls and merry laughter ringing through corridors. Servants had bustled to and fro, fires always blazing in the hearths to ward off the chill. Her father's jovial voice had boomed with joy and pride.

Now, only shadows and silence remained. Stripped of its finery and warmth, Riverwood stood as a husk of its former glory, ravaged by the cruel winds of fate. Like barren trees in the dead of winter, her family had been left exposed, their roots withering under the weight of scandal and ruin.

Charlotte's heart clenched as she recalled the happier days—whirling through the grand ballroom, her silk skirts sweeping the floor, her father's laughter filling the air as he twirled her about. She could still feel the warmth of the hearth, her family gathered around it, their faces aglow with love and contentment. The memory was too sweet, too painful.

It had all been ripped away by the cruel machinations of one man.

The memories cut through her—too sweet to bear, yet impossible to forget. Her chest tightened until she could scarcely breathe, and then the rage burned through her like fire, scalding away the numbness with its savage heat. She welcomed the anger. The flames of conviction that had settled over her in the wake of their downfall.

This would not be the end for her family. Not while she still had the strength to fight.

Charlotte lifted her chin, her eyes narrowing at the winter landscape beyond. Let the cold winds howl. She would weather the storm and emerge victorious, no matter the cost. Her gaze flicked to the portrait of her father above the mantel, his familiar features both a comfort and a painful reminder of all they had lost. A pang of guilt twisted in her chest as a painful weight settling upon her shoulders.

"Forgive me, Father," she murmured. "I should have done more."

But regret would not change their fate. Charlotte knew she had to look forward. She had a plan—one she had been crafting for months. The Duke of Ravenscroft, Grant Tilbury, thought himself untouchable, hidden behind his wealth and influence. But every man had weaknesses. She need only discover his. To that end, she had been carefully gathering information, piecing together rumors and whispered secrets.

He would pay for what he had done to her family. She would expose him. Society would see him for what he was—a villain masquerading as a nobleman.

Her fingers curled into fists at her sides, her nails biting into the soft flesh of her palms. She would not rest until she had completed her revenge. The Duke would pay for what he had done to her family.

She turned from the window, her skirts swishing softly as she left the cold shadows of the room. She made her way through the quiet, empty corridors, her footsteps echoing against the floorboards. Riverwood, like her family, had been stripped of its beauty.

She pushed open the sitting room door, then paused, her heart clenching at the sight that greeted her. Her mother, Lady Chatsworth, once a vibrant and lively woman, now sat hunched in a faded velvet armchair, her hands clenched tightly in her lap. Her once-rosy cheeks had hollowed, and the light in her eyes had dimmed. The room itself seemed to have lost its luster, the furniture worn and the draperies threadbare.

"Mama," Charlotte greeted softly, moving to sit beside her near the fire. "How are you feeling today?"

Mother glanced up, her weary gaze meeting Charlotte's. "I fear for our future, my dear," she sighed, her hands trembling in her lap. "The debts keep mounting, and we have had to let more staff go. I do not know how much longer we can hold on."

Charlotte squeezed her mother's hand, hoping to

impart some measure of strength. "We will find a way, Mama. I promise you."

Mother shook her head, a mirthless smile playing at the corners of her mouth. "Your optimism is admirable, my dear, but I fear it may be misplaced. We are on the brink of losing everything, and I cannot bear the thought of you and your brother suffering more than you already have for your father's mistakes."

The mention of her father ignited a fresh wave of anger, but Charlotte forced it down, focusing instead on comforting her mother. "I will not let that happen, Mama. I have a plan, and I will see it through. The Duke of Ravenscroft will not get away with what he has done to us."

"You think a plan will save us?" Her mother's voice wavered, the words more accusation than plea.

Charlotte hesitated, the protest caught in her throat. For a moment, doubt crept in, but she swallowed it down, her gaze hardening. "Yes, Mama. I have a plan," she said, the words slipping out like a vow. Her mind was already turning, piecing together the steps she would need to take—the secrets she would unravel, the alliances she might have to forge. But she kept those thoughts to herself, unwilling to risk a single misstep.

"Charlotte, you must not." Mother's eyes widened

as she gripped Charlotte's hand. "The Duke is powerful. I do not want you putting yourself in harm's way, or damaging your reputation. It is all you have left. Besides, your father is not without blame. If not for his actions—"

"I will be careful," Charlotte reassured her, though her resolve had already hardened. She would not back down, no matter the cost.

Lady Chatsworth studied her daughter's face for a long moment, as though searching for some sign of hesitation or doubt. Finding none, she let out a heavy sigh, her shoulders slumping in defeat.

"I suppose there is nothing I can say to dissuade you," she murmured, a hint of pride mingling with the worry in her tone. "You always were stubborn girl."

"I learned from you, Mama," Charlotte replied with a soft smile, remembering the countless times her mother had scolded her for her headstrong ways

For a brief moment, a spark of the woman Edith Ashbourne, Viscountess Chatsworth used to be flickered in her eyes, but it was quickly extinguished by the weight of their reality. "Just promise me you will not do anything foolish," her mother whispered. "I could not bear to lose you, too."

Charlotte leaned forward, pressing a gentle kiss

to her mother's forehead. "I promise, Mama. I will make things right."

A clatter of footsteps rang down the hall, interrupting them. Henry burst into the room, breathless, his cheeks flushed with excitement. The parchment in his hand shook as he held it out, his voice barely able to contain the thrill of whatever news he bore.

"Mother, Charlotte," he exclaimed, rushing toward them. "You will never believe what has arrived."

At thirteen years old, Henry was the epitome of youthful optimism, his boundless enthusiasm a stark contrast to the somber atmosphere that had settled over Riverwood Manor in recent months. Charlotte could not help but smile at his excitement, even as her heart ached at the thought of the burden he now carried as the Earl of Ashbourne.

"What is it, Henry?" she asked, reaching out to ruffle his unruly mop of blond hair. "What has come?"

He thrust the vellum toward her, his grin threatening to split his face in two. "It is your entry back into society. The first step in elevating our family once more. An invitation to the Duke of Ravenscroft's Christmas ball."

Charlotte froze, her gaze locked on the proffered invitation. Her fingers hovered over the heavy vellum, a chill running down her spine as she caught sight of the Duke's bold signature. The world seemed to narrow around her—the fire's crackle dimmed, her mother's soft gasp barely a whisper—as she read the name that had haunted her dreams. Grant Tilbury, Duke of Ravenscroft. The man who had single-handedly destroyed her family's fortune and reputation. The man she had sworn to bring to his knees.

And now, he had the audacity to invite them to his ball?

Mother let out a soft gasp, her hand flying to her mouth in shock. "The Duke of Ravenscroft? Inviting us to his ball? But why would he do such a thing, after everything he has done to us?"

Charlotte's mind raced with possibilities, each more sinister than the last. Was this some sort of cruel joke, a way for the Duke to flaunt his victory over them? Or perhaps it was a trap, a way to lure them into his clutches and finish what he had started. Was it not enough that he taken their money, their silver and jewels. He had caused them to sell off everything of value, leaving them destitute. They could no longer afford Henry's schooling and Father's heart had failed as a result of it all. What more could the devil possibly do to them?

A sudden realization dawned on her. This was it.

This was the opportunity she had been waiting for. The chance to put her plan for revenge into motion.

A slow smile spread across her face, her eyes glinting with a newfound tenacity. "Why, Mama," she said, her voice dripping with false sweetness, "it is simply an invitation to a ball. And who are we to refuse such a generous offer from His Grace?"

Henry's brow furrowed, not quite understanding the undercurrent of tension in the room. "So... does that mean you are going?" he asked, his voice hopeful.

Charlotte reached out and plucked the invitation from his hand, her fingers trembling slightly as they brushed against the heavy parchment. "Yes, Henry," she said, her gaze never leaving the elegant script that spelled out the Duke's name. "We are going. And I am going to show the Duke of Ravenscroft exactly what happens when you cross the Ashbournes."

Charlotte had never met the duke in person, but the rumors painted a vivid picture. They spoke of a man with a commanding presence, tall and broad-shouldered, with dark hair and grey eyes that seemed to see straight through to a person's soul. He was said to be devastatingly handsome, with a charm that could disarm even the most guarded of hearts.

But she knew that beneath his charming exterior, lay a heart of ice. The Duke was known for his ruthless business dealings, his ability to crush his enemies without a second thought. He had a reputation for being cold and calculating, always one step ahead of his opponents.

And now, he had wrought devastation on her family.

Charlotte's mother let out a weary sigh, pulling her from her thoughts. "Charlotte, my dear, I know you mean well, but I fear this may be a battle not worth fighting. The Duke is too powerful, too well-connected. What can you possibly do against him?" She reached for Charlotte's hand. "Would your time not be better spent looking for a husband?"

Charlotte shook her head. "No gentleman would have me now, and you well know it." She squeezed mother's hand. "But do not fret. We can fight, Mama. I can show him that our family is not to be trifled with. We may have lost Father, but we still have our pride, our dignity. And I will not let the Duke take that from us. We will attend the ball, along with any other social events we receive invitations to."

Mother's eyes filled with tears, and she pulled Charlotte into a tight embrace. "My brave girl," she whispered, her voice choked with emotion. "Your father would be so proud of you."

Charlotte blinked back her own tears, her resolve hardening with each passing moment. She rose from her seat, her heart heavy with the knowledge of what lay ahead. She would confront the Duke, expose his misdeeds, and restore her family's honor. But first, she needed to prepare.

Retreating to her chambers, Charlotte sat at her writing desk, her mind already racing with plans. She reached for a sheet of parchment, dipping her quill into the inkwell as she began a letter to Lady Arabella Fitzwilliam, her closest friend and confidante.

My dearest Arabella,

I write to you with a matter of great importance. The Duke of Ravenscroft has taken everything from my family, and I cannot stand by any longer. I have a plan to expose him, but I need your help. I fear I am short on gowns these days. Might you have one to loan me?

Ever yours, Charlotte

As she signed her name, doubt crept in. Was revenge truly the answer? Was this the path her father would have wanted her to take? Could she truly restore their name honor and fortune?

The thought of her father's broken spirit, the way

his life had ended, and her mother's despair pushed the doubt away.

With resolve hardening in her chest, Charlotte sealed the letter and sent it off with their only remaining footman. She stood by the window, watching the snow fall in soft, silent sheets against the moonlit sky as she considered her revenge.

She smiled at her reflection in the window glass. The Duke of Ravenscroft would soon learn the true meaning of retribution, and Charlotte would be the one to teach him that lesson.

"Grant Tilbury, Duke of Ravenscroft, you took everything from us," she whispered into the night. "Now I will take it back, and you will rue the day you dared to cross the Ashbournes."

Author's note

I have often heard it said that Christmas Trees were not in England during the Regency era. Leastwise, they were not a common occurrence. But that is poppycock!

The Regency era started in February 1811 and lasted until January of 1820. The Christmas tree was introduced to England, as a matter of record, during the Christmas season of 1800.

For the Christmas party, her majesty, Queen Charlotte hosted in 1800, she had a Yew tree potted and brought into Queen's Lodge. The queen had decorated the tree with sweetmeats, almonds and raisons in paper, toys and fruit, along with small wax candles. It was to be a special surprise for the children of the principle families in Windsor. And by all accounts, they were delighted.

As a result, Christmas trees became all the rage among upper class English families. A variety of trees were used for the purpose: box-trees, yews, pines, and furs among them, but one thing remained consistent: They were all lit with small candles and decorated with treats and other trinkets. It was also common to find a Regency Christmas tree with presents piled beneath its branches.

There are accounts of lords, earls, and dukes having Christmas trees in their homes as early as 1802 when George, second lord Kenyon, bought 'candles for his tree' that he erected in his drawing room at 35 Lincoln's Inn Field, London.

And by the time of Queen Charlotte's death in 1818, the tradition of having a Christmas tree was firmly rooted in English society.

I hope that you have enjoyed Emily and Nicolas's love story and will pick up the other books available in the Regency Hearts Aflame series.

Warmest wishes,
Amanda

About the Author

Amanda Mariel, an accomplished wordsmith, holds dual master's degrees in liberal arts and education, specializing in the captivating realms of history and literature. Beyond her academic pursuits, she embraces the joyful chaos of motherhood, tending to both her cherished teenagers and her trio of adored fur babies. Among them, a noble Bernese Mountain Dog named Blaze, and two cats of distinct character, Ezra and Puff, share their home.

A USA Today Bestselling luminary, Amanda Mariel conjures vivid tapestries of eras long past, drawing inspiration from the languid cadence of days gone by. With pen poised and imagination unfurled, she traverses the annals of time, weaving tales that illuminate historical landscapes with finesse and flair. Her creative spirit finds respite in reading, traversing new horizons through travel, and capturing moments through the lenses of both her camera and artistic endeavors. Yet, it is in the embrace of family that she finds her truest sanctuary.

To delve deeper into Amanda's captivating world visit www.amandamariel.com. While there, an invitation to join her newsletter promises a gateway to the latest from Amanda Mariel's literary treasury, and an opportunity to claim a complimentary eBook.

Amanda's passion extends to her readers, welcoming their voices and stories into her narrative realm. Engage with her through email at amanda@amandamariel.com, or connect via her social Media channels.

Facebook: facebook.com/AuthorAmandaMarie1
    Twitter: twitter.com/AmandaMarieAuth
    BookBub: bookbub.com/authors/amanda-mariel
    Instagram: instagram.com/authoramandamariel
    TicTok: tiktoc.com/@amandamarielromance

Amidst the prose and parchment, Amanda Mariel etches a profound connection, bridging eras, hearts, and minds, creating a legacy that resonates through the corridors of time.

Also by Amanda Mariel

Ladies and Scoundrels series

Scandalous Endeavors

Scandalous Intentions

Scandalous Redemption

Scandalous Wallflower

Scandalous Liaison

Dancing with Serendipity

Fabled Love Series

Enchanted by the Earl

Captivated by the Captain

Enticed by Lady Elianna

Delighted by the Duke

Lady Archer's Creed series

Amanda Mariel writing with Christina McKnight

Theodora

Georgina

Adeline

Josephine

Scandal Meets Love series

Love Only Me

Find Me Love

If it's Love

Odd's of Love

Believe in Love

Chance of Love

Love and Holly

Love and Mistletoe

A Rogue's Kiss Series

Her Perfect Rogue

His Perfect Hellion

This Rogue of Mine

Her Perfect Scoundrel

Wicked Earls' Club

Titles by Amanda Mariel

Earl of Grayson

Earl of Edgemore

Earl of Persuasion

Earl of Stone (Fated for a Rogue)

Fated for a Rogue

A Wallflower's Folly

One Fateful May Day

Fate Gave Me a Duke

Earl of Stone (Wicked Earls' Club)

Who Needs a Duke

Rogue for the Taking

Wish Upon a Christmas Duke

Scandalously Mine

A Castle Romance

Whispers of Desire

Passion's Lasting Promise

One Wanton Wager

Forever in Your Arms

Regency Heart's Aflame

So Long, My Scoundrel

Rogue Under the Mistletoe

All I Want for Christmas is a Rogue

Au Revoir, My Duke

Farewell, My Rogue

Duke of No Return

Courting Ruin

A Midsummer Night's Rendezvous

Connected by a Kiss

These are designed so they can standalone

How to Kiss a Rogue (Amanda Mariel)

A Kiss at Christmastide (Christina McKnight)

A Wallflower's Christmas Kiss (Dawn Brower)

Stealing a Rogue's Kiss (Amanda Mariel)

Scandalized by a Rogue's Kiss (Amanda Mariel)

A Gypsy's Christmas kiss (Dawn Brower)

A Vixen's Christmas kiss (Dawn Brower)

Standalone titles

One Moonlit Tryst

One Enchanting Kiss

Christmas in the Duke's Embrace

One Wicked Christmas

A Lyon in Her Bed (The Lyon's Den connected world)

Courting Temptation (House of Devon connected world)

Forever My Rogue (Love Be a Lady's Charm Connected World)

Box sets and anthologies

Visit www.amandamariel.com to see Amanda's current offerings.

Thank you so much for taking the time to read *All I Want for Christmas is a Rogue.*

Your opinion matters!

Please take a moment to review this book on your favorite review site and share your opinion with fellow readers.

∼

USA Today bestselling author

~Heartwarming historical romances that leave you breathless~

Milton Keynes UK
Ingram Content Group UK Ltd.
UKHW031617231124
451036UK00001B/11

9 798227 255341